HUNTER'S BABY

ALEXIS ABBOTT

PATHFORGERS PUBLISHING

Get an EXCLUSIVE book, **FREE** just as a thank you for signing up for my newsletter! Plus you'll never miss a new release, cover reveal, or promotion!

http://alexisabbott.com/newsletter

His muffled, panicked voice tries to cry out through the gag in his mouth as I tighten the robes binding him to the old maple tree. Once the knot is tight and secure, I stalk around the tree, peering at my victim through the eye holes in my ski mask. The last light of day fades behind me as I look into those terrified eyes, and I'm the last thing he sees in daylight before the night swallows us.

He is afraid, but he isn't in pain. He deserves pain, but that isn't how I operate. I'm not a sadist, or some maniac who gets off on torture. I do this because the way I see it, this is the right thing to do. What I'm doing is making the world a better place.

I look into his wide, bulging eyes as the fading light makes my reflection vanish from his pupils. My victim is a tall man with a clean-shaven face and angular features. He's skinny, but I know firsthand that he's stronger than he looks. He's an accountant. He looks nothing like the kind of monster I know he really is. The real monsters are rarely burly, terrifying men covered in scars and tattoos. The most deadly ones are the ones you'd never suspect.

"We're a long way out in the woods," I say calmly, listening to the sound of his quick, loud breathing. "Hear that waterfall? It's closer than you think." I reach for the sheath on my belt and pull out a long hunting knife. The metal makes a soft noise against the leather, and my victim tries to shout and struggle in his bindings. It's useless, of course. The knots I tied in that rope could hold down a grizzly bear. I twirl the knife in my hand and reach to his face to take hold of the cloth wrapped around his face, holding the gag in.

"Let's have a chat," I say, just as calm as ever, even though the man in front of me is thrashing wildly against the rope. All he's doing is giving himself rope burns. "You can scream all you want, but nobody's going to hear you out here. And if they knew what you've done, they wouldn't want to do anything about it anyway."

That gets his attention.

As I hook my fingers under the cloth and bring the razor-sharp knife to his face, I cut it loose, then pull the gag out of his mouth with my gloved hand. I'm dressed in a ski mask, a black sweater, dark jeans, and black hiking boots. I drop the nasty gag, and to my surprise, my victim doesn't start howling like a wounded animal as soon as he can. He watches me carefully, pale face sweaty and fearful.

I pull my mask off my face so we can look at each other like human beings, even though I'm not keen on calling him that. Immediately, his eyes start trying to memorize my features. I can almost read his mind, thinking about describing me to the police: a man with somewhat dark skin in his late twenties, brown hair and eyes, muscular, with a very short and trimmed beard, strong jaw and prominent brow, hair shaved on the sides and short on top. He might add broad shoulders and a deep voice that sounds like it's from somewhere around here upstate.

"What do you want?" he asks in a tired, scared voice. "Money? I've got a lot of money."

I don't answer. I stare into his eyes, searching him, wondering how far he'll go. After a few moments of silence, he keeps talking.

"Enough money to set up a guy like you real good. You like girls? I can hook you up with someone nice. Someone who won't put up a fight. I got a lot of friends who have a lot of handy skills, you know? I-I can make things happen. A lot of things. Is there some girl you've always wanted? I can make her yours. Let's...let's just talk about this, okay? Hell, I know some people who could put you to work. Make some real money. More than whoever's paying you for this. Someone's paying you, right? I'll double it. You get how this works, don't you? I pay you more, set you up with someone nice, and we get back at whoever's pulling the strings here. Make it so nobody ever knows what happened. That sounds good, right?"

He's amusing, I'll give him that.

His voice gets more desperate with every sentence. He's grasping at straws, but I don't think he realizes that. He thinks I'm a hitman, hired by some rival of his to take him out professionally. I'm flattered that he thinks I'm doing professional-grade work, frankly, and if I were, his string of absurd offers might have given me pause.

Men like him who only care about money will go to any lengths to climb higher on their mountains of vice.

"Do you...do you get what I'm offering?" he croaks, his voice almost pleading. He's trying to save some face, and it's laughable. "You hear me, right?" He pauses, eyes searching mine. "...how much do you know?"

I crack a smile at that.

"More than enough," I say, looking down at the blade of my knife and inspecting the edge. This tool of mine cuts through human skin like butter. I slowly pace over to the small bag I left a few feet away from us when I dragged my victim out into these woods southwest of Ithaca. Stooping down, I pull out a simple folder and open it, approaching him and thumbing through it.

"You've been a busy man, James," I say. Reviewing the folder in front of him is just for show. I've memorized every detail. "You don't fit the usual profile for your type. Most of you are happy to turn to white collar crime. But no, the second that you realized one of your clients had a hand in moving hard drugs, you wanted in. That's the kind of blackmail you usually see in hardened mafiosos."

His jaw sets as he watches me, and I can tell he's itching to try to say something to defend himself. But face to face with your own crimes with no justice system to hide under, it's hard to muster up a defense.

"You're not lying about being able to offer me women, though," I say, raising my glare to him. "You didn't spend much time helping drug traffickers cover their tracks. You figured out that there's just as much money in sex trafficking, with the bonus of being able to dip into your merchandise. You liked that. It went well for you, until one of the girls turned up dead."

He opens his mouth to say something, but he thinks better of it when he remembers the long knife in my hand. He was probably just about to try to call me a hypocrite for judging him, considering our circumstances. I always find that such a funny thing for these monsters to fall back on.

"Your mafia connections dropped you like a hot potato after that," I say, pacing slowly as I read over his crimes. "Let's be honest, if I hadn't gotten to you, they probably would have sent one of theirs after you eventually. But you didn't need the mafia. You'd already learned how to trap women. So you kept playing accountant for desperate people in poor neighborhoods. You found young women who were already desperate, and you took payment any way you wanted. And if they weren't to your liking, some of them had young daughters that you liked. *Very young daughters*," I add, shutting the folder and tossing it back down, approaching him, unable to keep the furious grimace off my face. "Even your own daughter, James? Your own flesh and blood? What's wrong with you?"

"Who *are* you?" he croaks, unwilling to acknowledge the crimes I have on him. "You don't look Russian. Italian? Who do you work for?"

I stare at him a long time before my full lips smile faintly.

"Don't know whether to be flattered or insulted," I say as I come to a stop right in front of him. "I'm neither. Just a concerned citizen." I put one gloved hand on his forehead, pushing it back against the tree and glaring at him in the eyes. "Standing up for the people who can't stand up for themselves."

"So you're a psychopath," he growls, straining his eyes to watch me.

"Not the word I'd use," I say, "but if you want that to be your last thought, you can have it."

Before he can reply, my right hand flashes up faster than the blink of an eye.

The next second, his eyes go wide, then slowly glass over as he makes a soft choking noise. I've plunged my knife straight through his neck to the wood behind him.

I always strike with surgical precision. It's quick, clean, quiet, and if all goes well, I sever the spinal cord with a single thrust, ending him quickly and painlessly. Normally, I don't even let them know what hit them. But I felt like this guy deserved to have his crimes put in front of him before he faces the devil in hell.

I hold the knife in place as I watch ruby-red blood start to pour from his wound. The groaning of the ropes around him tells me his body has gone limp. He's dead.

I leave the knife planted in his neck for a moment. I'll come back to it soon. I make my way over to my bag and take out the final piece of the scene I'm going to leave for the investigators that show up in a day or so.

It's a perfect white lilac, stored in a mason jar.

I take it out and move back to the victim's body, and I hold the lilac under the wound before I yank the knife out. Blood runs out from the wound and stains the white petals, tainting them with death. I carefully use the knife to open the victim's mouth, and I slide the flower stem into it, letting his teeth hold the bloodied flower in place, hanging out of his mouth.

I take a few steps back and survey my work.

One of the most evil men in Ithaca hangs limply from his bindings to an old tree up here on a rocky cliff in the woods. It's all brown and gray and a little leftover green out here, so the white lilac stained with drops of red blood stands out like the centerpiece of a painting on the scene. I have to admit, there's something beautiful about it.

I am a killer. That much is true. But I don't do it for the love of killing. I do it so that people like this man, who trap people, rape women, and destroy lives can't just walk freely like the rest of us. Men like him sniff out innocence and ruin it.

That's why the pure white lilac dipped in blood is my calling card.

The white lilac is a symbol of youthful innocence and memories, which is all I have left. A victim's blood stains it. It feels strange to leave a calling card, but it also feels right somehow, in a way I can't explain.

I leave the murder scene and gather up my things after carefully combing over the site to make sure there isn't a scrap of my DNA left to tie me to the crime. I gather up my bag and hike a ways away to an old cave that's too hard to get to for most vacationing hikers from the college. There, I set down the folder containing my victim's crimes, the gag I used to bind him, and every other incriminating piece of evidence I have. I strip down naked and add it to the pile before emptying a container of lighter fluid onto the pile. I put on the change of clothes from the sealed bag I brought with me, then strike a match and toss it onto the pile.

I step back and watch it all burn. I'm now wearing a hiker's outfit, and if anyone sees me coming out of the woods, I'll look like just another hiker who spent too much time in nature this evening. Not that anyone will see me up close. My route is carefully planned and shadowy.

As I watch the fires burn down to nothing but charred ashes and prepare to burn them again until there's nothing left, I can't stop thinking about her.

She's always on my mind when I make a kill.

There's one reason I do this. One reason I strike out into the world to hunt down the sociopathic, evil people who make it a dark place. I don't relish the act of killing, but I do relish the act of making the world a safer place...all for her.

My innocence was stolen away, too. Like the snow-white petals of the lilac flower forever stained in red blood before being doomed to wilt away, innocence can't be taken back. Once it's gone, that box can't be closed again. It's a tragedy that almost all of us must go through, whether we like it or not.

For many people, it's a violent process that leaves you shaken and traumatized for the rest of your life.

It certainly did for me. My mind races with worries over whether I spent too much time talking to my latest victim, but when it comes to parents abusing their children, it strikes far too close to home for me to resist forcing them to confront their crimes before I end it. I still wake up in a cold sweat sometimes, the sounds of my parents' angry voices ringing in my ears, moments before one of their hands came down hard on me. That's something I'm going to live with forever, just like James's daughter will live with it forever, no matter how just his death is. Abuse is a wound that keeps on bleeding.

I wonder what that means for me, standing here in a fresh set of clothes and getting covered in the smell of smoke as I watch the last traces of my crime burn before my eyes. Does the question of right and wrong even matter? I don't pretend I'm a good man. I'm an evil man trying to do good.

All for her.

The yellow fire reminds me of her blonde hair. It's so soft that I can almost feel it against my finger-tips again. If I lose myself in the hypnotic sight of the flames, I can almost take myself back to that place I haven't been with her for so, so long. Her naked body against mine, our warmth together, our lips pressed tight together, her scent in my nose...she is like no other.

She's still out there, too. I wonder what she's doing tonight. I don't even know where she is. All I can hope is that she's happy, and the only way I can make that come true is if I make the world a better place...removing one sorry sack of shit at a time.

All for her.

All for Blossom.

"Hi! Welcome to the Lazy Bean. How are you doing today?" I chirp brightly as the next customer in line moves up to the cash register. My cheeks are aching from hours and hours of holding this same plastered, probably unconvincing smile on my face, but I know I have to keep it up for a little while longer. After all, my strict manager is the one on duty today. All day long I've felt his prickly presence behind me, hovering while I try to do my job. You would think we're some high security clearance team working at the Pentagon or something, Marty is so uptight. It's just an upscale coffee shop, but he runs the place like every latte or pastry order is of life-or-death importance. I guess that's why he's the manager and I'm just a lowly barista; he gives way more of a damn than I do. But to be honest, I would be a lot more enthusiastic about my job if I was making much more per hour.

The customer, a middle-aged woman wearing designer sunglasses indoors (presumably to show off the word GUCCI emblazoned in tiny silver lettering on the frame), scoots up, leans her elbow on the counter, and replies in a conversational tone, "I'm okay, hon. Could be better. It's awfully windy out there, huh?"

Ah, great. A chatty Cathy. Just what I need when the line is nearly out the door.

But I can positively feel Marty's eyes boring into the back of my head from across the kitchen area behind the counter, so I just hoist the edges of my smile a little bit higher and lean in. It's just after four o'clock in the afternoon. I just have three more hours left to survive and then I get to go home and spend the rest of the night decompressing from work. And frowning as much as I want to, of course.

"Oh, is it windy?" I ask. "I haven't been out there since six-thirty this morning, and it was pretty calm outside then."

"Six-thirty?" the woman replies, letting out a low whistle. "Boy, that's awfully early. You must be one of those natural early-risers. Ha. Not me! I don't get out of bed before at least eleven, not unless my bed is on fire!"

She starts cackling at her own joke and I hurriedly force myself to chuckle along with her as she slaps the counter with her palm, apparently just totally tickled by her own sense of humor. She's a little obnoxious, but I remind myself it could be much worse. She could be a mean customer or a rude customer or an impatient customer. All of which I see every single day here. You'd think handing people delicious beverages would precipitate a more pleasant work environment. I mean, this isn't the DMV or anything. And if you're a customer here, especially a regular, then your life must be pretty sweet. Anyone who can afford a six-dollar cup of coffee on a daily basis is clearly operating in a much higher echelon of society than I am. And yet, so many people roll through this cafe in such sour moods every day. I don't get it. If I had that kind of financial stability and freedom...well, let's just say I wouldn't take it for granted.

"Anywho, I'm just dying for a latte," says the woman. She pinches the bridge of her designer shades and lowers them slightly so she can squint up over my shoulder at the menu on the wall. Oh. She's one of *those* types who doesn't seem to decide what she wants until she's already at the register, even though she's had a good five minutes standing in line to peruse the menu. I decide to offer some suggestions to try and move her along, as the line is only growing longer and longer and the people behind her look increasingly impatient.

"What type of latte? Hot or iced? What sort of

flavors do you usually go for?" I ask helpfully. She scratches at her chin and tilts her head from one side to the other.

"Hmm," she contemplates. I have to grip the underside of the counter to let out some of my own pent-up annoyance and impatience. I wish I could tell her, *Look, lady, I've got a whole line of people standing behind you who know exactly what they want. Just make a decision already before they all decide to start a mutiny and kill us both.* But instead I just smile beatifically and watch her hem and haw over the menu.

"What's that new pink latte I keep seeing ads for everywhere? Looks like strawberry or cherry blossom or something, I think," the woman asks curiously.

"That'll be our rose-cardamom latte. It was just supposed to be a promotional flavor for spring back in April, but it was such a hit we decided to keep it for the rest of the year. Would you like to try that today?" I press her, my words stumbling over each other in my haste to get through this damn transaction.

"What does cardamom taste like?" she asks, leaning more heavily on the counter and peering up at me with brown eyes behind her shades.

Oh, good god. Is this is a game of twenty questions? How can one woman take up so much space and time? Is this really happening right now? All the customers behind her are glaring daggers at me as if it's my fault that little Miss Gucci Shades has decided to move in and start paying rent at my cash register or whatever. But I must be strong.

"Cardamom is kind of complex. It's a little spicy, a little sweet, kind of citrusy-- and some people say it's sort of minty, but I don't taste that at all," I explain. I've rolled out this exact description probably a hundred times already. It's like a rehearsed speech at this point.

"Spicy? Hmm. I don't know about spicy," she murmurs.

"It's not super spicy," I backtrack, feeling my heart sink as my attempt to sell her on it seems to be failing. "It's really good. I promise."

She raises an eyebrow and looks at me hard, like she's sizing me up to determine whether I'm telling her the truth. As if this is the most life-changing decision one could ever make. Then, to my mingled relief and exasperation, she replies, "Eh, I think I'll just get a large iced pumpkin latte with soy milk."

"Oh. Okay! Yes, ma'am. Coming right up. That'll be five-sixty-two, please," I remark, my fingers flying across the buttons on the screen. As I'm ringing her up, part of my mind seems to function on autopilot while another part of my brain drifts away to focus on the music filtering out of the radio station playing softly over the cafe speakers. It's one of those easy-listening indie stations, generally playing the kind of music that makes me want to lie down and take a nap. I always wonder if Marty picks that station to balance out the caffeinated energy of the customers. As if playing a rap song or a rock song would send our jittery customers into a mosh pit and start wrecking the interior design here. I finish ringing up my garrulous customer just as the final twangy notes of the current acoustic song fades out and is followed by a radio DJ announcing in a cheesy, soft voice that there's a breaking new development in a suspicious crime wave striking Albany. At first I try to tune it out, assuming it's just another electronics shop being robbed or some little old lady getting mugged-- the usual unfortunate but less-than-intriguing fare you tend to hear about when you live in a metropolitan area like this one in upstate New York. But then, I hear a string of words that immediately captures all of my attention and makes my blood run cold.

"This is a Smooth Listening One-oh-Five-Point-Nine news exclusive. Police witnesses have shared the news that there has been a body discovered in Ithaca, New York. Yes, that's right, dear listeners. A body. As yet unidentified, but it looks to be possibly some sort of contract killing. The victim, whose name has not been released, seems to have been stabbed through the neck with a surgical instrument, perhaps. The police are calling it a random murder at this time, but rest assured, Smooth Listeners, that we will be providing updates as more information from Ithaca PD trickles in. Be careful out there, folks! Stay safe and, as always, stay smooth," croons the DJ in his artfully sleepy voice.

After that brief bulletin, another song starts back up, but it's too late. I'm totally lost in thought, my heart pounding like crazy. I feel tingly all over and enraptured by the startling news. I glance around, frowning to see that nobody else seems to have even paid the least bit of attention to the breaking news. Is the discovery of a murdered body really not very interesting to these folks? Are they truly more interested in gossiping and sipping fancy macchiatos to care that a man has been brutally killed in a city not so far from here?

The cogs in my brain are already churning faster and faster as I contemplate the sparse details of the murder. Stabbed through the neck? A supposed contract killing? And yet also a random murder? I want to roll my eyes at how silly it sounds. How could a contract killing ever be random? It's the opposite of random by the very nature of the reason for committing the crime. It's something done for a reason. Maybe not always (or ever) a good reason, but still. I can't stop fixating on the conflicting information, trying to make sense of it so that maybe at some point in the near future, when or if I get a little slice of precious free time, I might be able to cover this case on my new, fledgeling true crime podcast...

"Blossom!" barks a gruff, demanding male voice,

the source of which seems to be mere inches from my ear. I am so startled that I let out a little yelp of fear and whip around to face my manager, Marty Driscoll, who's looming over me with a red, scrunched-up, grumpy face that will eternally remind me of a slobbery bulldog.

"Y-Yes, sir?" I stammer, blinking rapidly as I try to jolt my brain back to the present moment. I realize with a sinking feeling that there's a long, long line forming all the way out the doors. Who knew four in the afternoon would be such a popular hour for people seeking a boost of caffeine?

"You have a customer! Stop daydreaming and do your damn job. you still have three hours left on your shift. You can listen to the news on your own time, not mine," Marty scolds.

I nod vigorously, feeling sick to my stomach. I've never dealt very well with harsh criticism, especially when men raise their voices. After the upbringing I had, it's just one of those things that always makes me tremble.

"Yes, sir. My apologies. I-I'll do better," I insist, turning to serve my next customer with my cheeks burning beet red.

"Good," grumbles Marty as he waddles away, presumably to browbeat someone else.

I look up at my customer with the same forced smile I always wear as part of my work uniform along with my name tag and my apron, but my smile falters when I see his face. He's a middle-aged man, probably in his late forties or early fifties, with salt-and-pepper hair, beady black eyes, and what I assume to be a perpetual scowl. He looks at me like I might as well be a servant or perhaps a dairy cow who's failing to produce milk. Instantly, I feel uncomfortable. It's like those shrewd, squinty little eyes are trying to bear down into my soul and extract my deepest fears and insecurities. I know his type immediately, instinctively. He hates women, all women, but especially the young and pretty ones like me.

That's right, I'm not oblivious. I know I've got a nice figure and a pleasant face. Add to that my big blue eyes and wavy blonde hair pulled back into a peppy ponytail, and I know I must look like the epitome of this guy's favorite prey.

"I'm so sorry for keeping you, sir. I got a little distracted, I guess," I tell him, nervously fiddling with the lanyard around my neck. "So, what can I get started for you today?"

"Aren't you going to ask me how my day is going?" he growls.

I blink in surprise for a moment, then it dawns on me that I had asked Miss Chatty Cathy how her day's been, and apparently this guy is offended I didn't offer him that same tepid, pointless greeting. So I yank my smile up a little wider and ask, "How *is* your day going, sir?"

"Well, it was alright until I got here, to be honest with you, Miss," he grumbles. "You might want to learn how to pay attention if you want to keep your job. Not every customer is going to be as forgiving as I am."

Ugh. The nerve. Keep your cool, Blossom, it's just a paycheck...

"Oh. I'm sorry to hear that. I'll do my best to ensure the rest of your time here at the Lazy Bean goes smoothly. What would you like to drink today? And what name would you prefer for the order?" I prattle off, scribbling the name *Ronald* on a cup and going onto autopilot so that I don't climb over the counter and claw the bastard's eyes out.

I put in his order as fast and accurately as possible, and I heave a sigh of relief when he moves on down to wait at the end of the barista counter for his drink. But as I'm serving the next customer, I see out of the corner of my eye that the jerk is clearly complaining about me to Marty! Shit. Shit, shit shit. That can't be good.

A few moments later, Marty sidles up next to me and growls into my ear, "I just gave that man his drink for free, but it's coming out of your paycheck. Remember that next time."

I'm pissed off, but there's nothing I can do except nod. I scramble through the next several orders until, finally, it's time for my break. As usual, I prepare myself a free cup of coffee behind Marty's back, and then hurry out the back to the little patio where we all like to hide out for smoke breaks. I don't smoke, but I do love getting ten minutes to myself to stand outside and breathe the fresh air. Although, I'm not sure just exactly how fresh the air here is in the city, but it's better than being cooped up in the Bean all day with no interruptions. I'm twenty-three, a single mom living in a strange city that still doesn't always feel like home. I'm from a small town originally, so sometimes I do struggle with the faster, more impatient pace of life here. I do find my little ways to ground myself and entertain the curiosity I've had since I was a child.

I stand there, bouncing up and down on the balls of my feet and using the hot coffee cup to keep my hands warm in the autumn breeze. Luckily, I have a long-sleeved shirt and jeans under my work apron, so I'm not too chilly out here. I look up and down the narrow alley, waiting for my usual encounter. Everyone thinks I'm a sucker, but to be honest, I kind of look forward to my brief chats with the clever, spunky homeless girl who usually meets up with me during my afternoon break.

Just like clockwork, she comes strolling around the corner. I give her a smile and a wave and she responds with a cool, aloof nod. Her name is Samantha Monroe, and she's only eighteen, a whole year younger than my little sister, but she's been on the streets for two years now after getting kicked out of her parents' house. I still have never managed to ask her exactly what happened with her folks, but I figure if she hasn't told me yet, there's probably a reason she doesn't want me to know. The young girl walks up to the patio and leans back on the railings, dressed in a ratty old sweater with holes at the elbows and ripped jeans. Her shoes look like they might fall apart at any moment. I hand her the coffee, which she accepts with a big smile.

"Medium roast this time. Should be a little less bitter," I tell her.

"Thanks, B. I really needed this today," she replies, taking a sip.

"Are you cold?" I ask, looking at her less-than-ideal outfit. She shrugs.

"Eh. Not really. I keep moving all day, so that keeps me warm," Sam says.

I bite my lip. "Hey, look. Have you heard about what happened in Ithaca?" I ask.

She frowns and shakes her head. "Nah. What happened?"

I lower my voice and explain, "The cops found a body."

"A dead one?" she clarifies.

I nod. "Yes. A dead body. What other kind would they find?"

She chuckles and shrugs. "Girl, I don't know. Sometimes when I'm sleepin' on a park bench people call the cops on me, too. I'm a body. But I'm not a dead one."

I smile-- the first genuine smile all day. "Okay. Fair enough. But anyway, I want you to be careful, alright? The police are saying it's a random homicide, but around here, that could mean anything. I worry about you being on the streets. Might make you an easier target."

She nods slowly. "I know. But I'm smart. I take care of myself, B. I'll be fine. Don't you worry about me. You got your own baby to worry about, eh?"

I laugh. "Yeah, I suppose that's right. But Flora doesn't sleep on park benches. I'm a little less concerned about a murderer getting to her."

Sam reaches over and pats my shoulder. "Seriously. I'll be okay. It's just one homicide all the way over in Ithaca. Big whoop. We live in the state of New York, B. There are murderers everywhere."

"Well, that's comforting," I sigh.

She giggles and gives me a look much wiser than her years as she starts going down the stairs to leave. "Take care of yourself, girl. I've got to go. Don't want Big Bad Boss-Man to come out here and bitch you out for giving out free coffee to the riff-raff like me," she says, winking at me over her shoulder.

After she disappears around the corner, I head back inside to finish out my shift. It goes by uneventfully, and at long last I get to clock out, whip off my stupid apron, and get in my car to go home.

As soon as I start up the engine, I hook up my phone to the stereo to play my most favorite guilty pleasure: a true crime podcast. I've been listening to them for years now, hungrily devouring all the crime-related content I can find. My sister, Sage, says it's a little morbid of me to be so intrigued by this stuff, but I can't help it. And over the years, she's starting to come around. In fact, I think I might be able to even get her to co-star on my own podcast with me. She may not be as interested in true crime as I am, but she *does* love to listen to herself talk. I know a podcast may sound like a pretty silly endeavor to some, but I don't want to be a barista forever. My dream goal is to become a journalist, and I think that starting my own podcast would be a great way to break into the industry.

To my excitement, I find that the podcast I'm listening to just uploaded a mini-episode discussing the murder in Ithaca. I listen with rapt attention as I drive home, catching all the little details. My heart stops as I hone in on one little detail the other report left out...

"There's only been one murder attributed to this guy so far, but we personally suspect he's going to be a prolific serial killer, so we've dubbed him 'The Gardener.' Why that name, you may ask? Well, the answer is simple. He left a calling card at the scene of the grisly murder: a white lilac, dipped in the victim's own blood."

Suddenly, it's like a memory I've kept sealed in a vault for five years comes springing at me out of the darkness. The sensation of sitting in the dewy grass, holding hands with the boy I loved, cuddling and kissing under the fragrance and shade of a white lilac bush that used to grow tall and impressive in a park down the road from my childhood home. Memories of his lips pressed against mine, his fingers interlocking with my own, as we whiled away the blissful hours together, wrapped up in young love. Memories of the young man I figured I'd never see again.

The man who remains the unknowing father of my child.

I can still remember just what it feels like to have the whole world ripped out from underneath you in a moment. How hard it is to reconcile the new life you're being forced to live with the twisted but beautiful life you were living before. It was never perfect, of course, and there were times when my old life was nigh unbearable. I grew up in a small town in northern Maine, the kind of place with only one stop light and endless fields of wavy green and wildflowers. The winters are long and sparkly white with snow and ice, while the warmer months are filled with dragonflies, chirping birds, and lush gardens. The rocky coastline can strike awe into the hearts of even the most jaded world traveler. There are lots of farms and quiet cottages tucked away from the rest of civilization, down long and winding dirt roads. It's a picturesque place to call home. That much I can't argue against.

But there's a downside to living in humble, rural isolation. Everybody knows each other. Everybody remembers your name and who you're related to. They remember what role you played in your fifth grade Christmas play. Your roots grow deep and people get stubborn about their homes and their ways. Change comes about slowly, and anyone who doesn't fall right in line with the way of things will stand out like a sore thumb. Luckily— or unluckily, depending on who you ask— I tended to be pretty damn good at blending in. After all, that's the way I was taught to behave. Girls are meant to be quiet and soft and obedient. They're supposed to be helpful without being asked, and speak only when spoken to. My mother was always the paragon of feminine virtue I aspired to. She's demure and diminutive and always, always dressed like she's going to church. Specifically, like she's going to church in the 1950s. Fluffy blonde hair, poofy sleeves, floor-length floral dresses, beige heels. She's the domestic goddess, queen of cooking, cleaning, and child-resting. Supposedly.

My father was the disciplinarian. The tall, imposing man in a dark jacket who went off to work with his briefcase and a cigarette and came home in the evenings with five o'clock shadow, an aching back, and a scowl. I lived to be helpful back then. I'd bend over backwards for even the most begrudging word of praise from my father. My sister Sage, who's four years younger than me, has always been the rebel. Even when I was seventeen and she was thirteen, I was the one cooped up at home all the time while she was sneaking out our bedroom window to meet boys. She never got caught, thankfully, but she confided in me about her adventures. She was brave and reckless enough to do the things I was too timid to do. I didn't dare step outside the lines, so I lived vicariously through Sage until that fateful summer when I turned eighteen.

It was the hottest summer northern Maine had seen in years. Record hot temperatures every day. I had just graduated high school— being home-schooled by my mother alongside my sister. I was looking into colleges on the down low, even though my parents didn't want me leaving our "safe" small town for university. It was understood that my future was going to involve a chapel wedding and probably six rowdy kids with some boring farmer across the way. I didn't want that life. I was itching for more.

I met Hunter at that crossroads in my life. He was the troubled, older guy who'd been in and out of foster homes most of his life. A hard worker and a good soul, but understandably rough around the edges. One day while I was out picking wild blackberries by the lilac trees on the edge of our six-acre property, I saw a man jump the fence and go running by, being chased by the farmer who owned the gigantic adjacent field. Apparently Hunter had stolen some produce from the farmer's crops and gotten caught. Although I was frightened, something inside me knew I could trust him. I helped Hunter hide under the lilac bush. Because of my pure and clean reputation, the farmer believed me and moved on. From then on out, Hunter and I would meet as often as we could at the edge of the field. We would lie underneath the lilac bush and eat sticky purple blackberries and talk about how much we hated our small town. At first, I thought we were just friends—that a handsome tough guy like Hunter could never be into a boring farm girl like me. But over the weeks of summer, we got closer and closer.

He was my first kiss.

Hell, he was my first everything. Right there under the lilacs, moonlight beaming down through the leafy branches. But we were too in love to be cautious, and I got pregnant.

As soon as my parents found out, they were enraged. The four of us left Maine for Albany, NY. Finally, Sage and I could get a taste of our big city dreams, but it wasn't so sweet. It was bitter. I didn't miss my hometown, but I was desperately heart-broken over Hunter. My parents broke off all contact between us. He never even knew I was preg-nant with his child, a fact which still haunts me.

They sent me away—they said it was for my own good, but I know it was just a cruel punishment. I was never able to find Hunter, no matter how hard I searched. It was like he never existed. And in the depths of my confusion and sadness, sometimes I could almost convince myself he never did—except that I have my daughter Flora as a constant reminder that he did exist. Especially because with her dark curls and brown eyes, she resembles her father so much.

Anyway, as soon as I was free, I cut my parents out of my life completely. I was finally old enough and independent enough and done with their toxic crap. I moved out without warning and didn't share my address with them. Sage did the same. She moved in with me to an apartment in Albany partly to escape our parents and partly to help me with the baby, Flora. (And partly because she and I have always been very close.) We get by. I work long hours at the Lazy Bean and Sage watches her niece at home. But Flora just started school now that she's five, so soon Sage will get a job, too, to help out. I want more than just to scrape by, though. I want to thrive. More specifically, I want to prove that I can thrive (and that Flora can thrive) without my parents' help. I have to prove that we don't need them.

Which is partially why we're all in the car together on this drizzly Saturday morning, driving the three hours from Albany to Ithaca. I want to investigate the lilac murder for my new podcast. If I want to get into crime journalism, I've got to start somewhere, right? And maybe it's a little crazy to be taking Sage and little Flora along with me on this wild goose chase, but I couldn't exactly justify leaving them at home. Besides, our landlord is finally having someone come paint our apartment this weekend, and we can't be trapped there with all the fumes. Especially not my little girl. So, it's off to beautiful, possibly deadly Ithaca for an impromptu weekend retreat. Sage and Flora are in the back seat, singing silly songs and playing little games to keep Flora occupied. I'm very fortunate that my daughter has always been so well-behaved; long car rides don't bother her as long as she has music to sing along with and lots of pretty scenery to point out. So far, we've gone through three CDs of children's movie soundtracks, and she's enthusiastically pointed at cows and horses and flowers out the car window. The scenery along the 79 is serene and beautiful, if a little empty.

"How's it going back there?" I ask, peering up at the rear view mirror. Flora is bouncing happily in her booster seat, flipping through the cardboard pages of a kids' book. I smile proudly, feeling my heart get warm at the sight of her. Only five years old and already reading like a champ. I mostly have Sage to thank for that. She's the best auntie imaginable, spending hours and hours every day doing little lessons with Flora. Sometimes I try to pay her for her efforts but she won't accept money from me. She just reminds me that in our little homeschool circle, I was the one who helped her learn to read— not our mother. So she sees it as collateral. I can't argue with that.

"We're great. Flora's reading her caterpillar book like a big girl and I'm just counting cows. Lots and lots of cows," Sage informs me with a grin.

"Yeah. It's pretty, isn't it?" I reply.

"Mhm. Reminds of home. Except without the, you know, horribly oppressive parents and that one town drunk who used to puke on our lawn every other Friday night. Other than that it's exactly the same," Sage says sardonically.

I can't help but snort a laugh at her description. It's spot-on. "Well, soon we're going to get some variety out there. We're well on our way toward the city now. Thanks for being so patient back there," I tell her. She shrugs good-naturedly.

"No problem. It's actually nice to get out of the apartment for a while. Don't get me wrong, I love staying in and taking care of Flora while you're at work, but it does get kind of boring sometimes," she says.

"Hey! I not boring," Flora protests, her pouty bottom lip poking out. I have to stifle a giggle at how precious she looks. Sage jumps to backtrack on her statement.

"No, no, baby girl. You're not boring at all. Auntie Sage just likes to get out of the house sometimes and see something new. Don't you?" she asks gently.

Immediately Flora's back to grinning. My heart surges to see that little gap-toothed smile. She just lost her first baby tooth, the left front one, last week. She was ecstatic to get a quarter under her pillow from "the tooth fairy."

"Yeah! I see flowers! Like Flora!" she exclaims, kicking her little feet excitedly.

"Yep. Like Flora," Sage agrees, giving me a wink. Ever since we taught her what her name means, she's been kind of obsessed with it.

"So, not to pry behind the journalistic curtain or whatever," Sage begins, leaning forward to talk to me. "But what exactly do you plan on doing when we get to Ithaca?"

"Oh, I just want to scout out the area for myself and maybe ask around for information. See if I can drum up any reluctant witnesses or something. Take notes. Some photos of the crime scene or as close to it as I can get. Nothing too crazy," I answer.

"You really think you're gonna be able to find witnesses even the police couldn't find?" she asks, raising an eyebrow.

"Who knows? I have a trustworthy face," I chuckle. "Maybe people will open up to me."

"Oh, sis. You've always been the one to think the best of people," Sage remarks fondly. "I wish I had that much optimism about people."

"Are you saying I'm naive?" I ask half-jokingly.

"Hey, you said it. Not me," she laughs. "Look, just promise you won't go sniffing up the wrong tree, okay? If the cops catch wind that you're snooping around a crime scene they might not like that very much."

"I know, I know. I'll be cautious. I'm not a private detective or anything, just a curious civilian," I reply brightly.

"Yeah," she sighs, shaking her head bemusedly, "that's what I'm worried about."

I steer the conversation back toward all the fun stuff we can do in Ithaca, offering to take them to a museum or the botanical gardens or even the nearby Ithaca Falls. This gets the both of them pretty pumped, as Sage looks up the attractions on her phone and shows pictures to Flora. The little girl is over the moon with excitement by the time our car rolls through the city limits. Where we were surrounded by greenery and emptiness before, now there are tall buildings and gorgeous city streets with shopping boutiques and interesting architecture on all sides.

I let the two of them ooh and ahh over the passing landmarks, turning my own attention back to my mission at hand. I really, really want to investigate this murder. But I'd be lying if I said my curiosity was piqued solely by the location of the murder and its suitability as the first episode of my podcast. No. It's more than that. I know it's silly, which is why I haven't shared this thought with my sister, but part of me is drawn to this homicide because of the unusual calling card.

The white lilac.

As soon as I heard about the white lilac stained with the victim's blood, I was hooked. I can't help it. I immediately flash back to that glorious summer back in Maine. The summer when I fell in love with the mysterious father of my child. When we rolled together, smiling and laughing under the pure white blooms of the lilac bush. We conceived Flora there—which is a big reason as to why I named her Flora.

It just seems like such a coincidence to me. I know Sage is right: that sometimes I can be a little naive, a little fixated. But whether or not the homicide has anything to do with Hunter, I can't help but be intrigued. It feels like I'm opening a door that has been locked shut for five years, finally taking a peek inside.

It's crazy. I know.

As I drive through the sluggish Ithaca traffic looking for a place to park, I hear my daughter ask a strange question she's never asked before. One that stuns me with its relation to my own thoughts right now.

"Sage, how come I no have a daddy?"

I look up at the rear view mirror just as Sage looks up to me, and we exchange tense expressions. Some wordless understanding passes between us. She turns to Flora and says in a deceptively cheerful voice, "Oh, you do have a daddy. He's just not here. But that's okay, because you have a mommy and an auntie right here who love you more than anything in the whole world."

Flora nods and smiles, but as she turns to look out the window, I think I catch a flicker of something like sadness on her sweet, chubby little face that breaks my heart.

When I turn my eyes back to the road in front of me, my heart nearly stops. There's something—someone—walking across the Main Street. A figure I would recognize anywhere, in any time, in any situation. The drizzling rain can't obscure him. I know with every thump of my heart that the man crossing in front of me, walking toward a coffee shop, is *him*.

After all these years, it's him. The man I've been looking for. The man whose shape I've chased through a crowd, whose voice has caught on the wind from time to time to remind me to always stay vigilant, on the off chance we might meet again someday.

Right in front of me.

In the middle of downtown Ithaca, in the last place I've thought to look, is Hunter.

I should already be gone.

That thought goes through my head every time I have to stick around somewhere longer than planned, and that happens almost every time I'm out on one of these jobs. Ithaca is a nice place, so the scenery sure doesn't leave me itching to get on the road back up to Maine as fast as possible. But every second I spend here is another second I risk getting caught doing what I consider my duty, and if that happens, it's all over. Sure, I have contingency plans. If I catch wind that I'm being followed by the wrong people, I can have a new identity and be over the Canadian border in less than twenty-four hours.

But I'd rather not have to resort to all that.

"Black coffee," I ask the barista at the coffee shop. "Large."

"That'll be $3.21, and can I get a name for the order?"

I open my mouth to give one of the many fake names I've given out over the years to cafes like this, but a voice behind me makes every cell in my body come to a halt.

"Hunter?"

For a solid five seconds, I am frozen, staring through the barista with a blank expression on my face. It can't be. Can it? I would know that voice anywhere, but it's impossible. There's just no way. Am I having some kind of hallucination? I'm not taking any meds, and last time I checked, I didn't need any. It must be a coincidence. She's been on my mind lately, so I shouldn't be surprised that my mind is playing tricks on me, making me hear what I want to hear deep down.

But I can't just ignore it. I know damn well I can't. So finally, I tear my eyes away from the barista to glance over my shoulder, expecting to see a stranger getting the attention of some other customer named Hunter.

Instead, I see *her*.

"Blossom…?"

That moment feels like an eternity. Blossom, the girl from my past, the girl who got taken away from me when we needed each other most, stands right there behind me. It has been five years. Five long years since the two of us saw each other. I was twenty-three, she was just eighteen. If I'm really looking at her and not hallucinating or having some kind of out-of-body experience, then the years have been incredible to her. She looks more beautiful than ever. Her blue eyes, her full lips, her long hair, every part of her looks just like I remember, but every little change she's made to herself over the years makes a hundred questions come to my head.

I'm stunned.

She breaks the spell between us by letting go of the child's hand and stepping forward to wrap her arms around me.

Wait, child?

I was so caught up in Blossom that I barely noticed the little girl holding her hand. On reflex, my body meets Blossom's hug in a tight one of my own, and we embrace right there in the coffee shop, feeling just like we did in the past. Over her shoulder, I see the child looking up at me with innocent curiosity. She doesn't look much like Blossom, but she has some traces of her there. The girl's hair is dark and curly, and her eyes are brown, but she has Blossom's nose and mouth. They must be related somehow.

Behind her is another familiar face-- it's Sage, Blossom's little sister. She was just fourteen when I saw her last, and a person changes a lot in those years, but it couldn't be anywhere else. She has the kind of face that doesn't change that much over time. She's looking at me with almost as much shock as I feel.

I'm so overwhelmed by the whole experience that I almost forget how much time is passing in our hug. We finally break apart, and I'm beyond happy to see a smile on Blossom's shining, beautiful face. She opens her mouth to say something more, but she glances behind me.

"...sir?"

The barista is looking at me with an apologetic smile, but I smirk back at him and reach into my pocket. I take out a crisp $50 and lay it on the counter.

"Their orders are on me," I say, nodding back to Blossom and the others. "The rest is for the tip jar."

The barista's face brightens, and I step aside to let Blossom and Sage put in their orders, but Sage steps forward to take the child's hand, giving Blossom a knowing smile.

"Hey, I know what you usually get, I'll take care of the orders," she says. "Why don't the two of you get us a table?"

"I-" Blossom starts to protest, but it doesn't take her long to give in, blushing and grinning. "That sounds great, actually, thanks." Turning to me, she raises her eyebrows and smiles, nodding to an empty table near a window. "Shall we?"

I can't believe that I'm crossing a busy coffee shop with Blossom. This can't be real. I start to wonder if this is all some afterlife experience, and that my last victim actually managed to kill me somehow. But when I sit down across from Blossom and look her in the eyes, seeing the sunlight outside crack through the rainy clouds just to cast some bright, natural light in those deep blue eyes...I know it's real.

We just look at each other for a moment, smiles on both our faces, no words being spoken. She's doing the same thing to me that I'm doing to her-- watching, taking in the way an old friend looks, letting all the feelings and questions bubble up to the fronts of our minds.

"I can't believe-"

"Oh my god-"

We try to speak at the same time, stop, and we can't help but laugh at ourselves. Just like that, it feels like we never left each other. Five long years threaten to melt away and take us back in time. And in the same moment, I realize that I haven't actually had a good, honest laugh in a long time. Hell, I can't remember the last time I've even smiled like this.

"You first," I say at last, quick enough to avoid doing the same thing. Blossom tucks a lock of hair behind her ear as her pink blush settles down.

"Gosh, I...how long has it been, Hunter?"

"Five years," I say, hardly able to believe it myself.

"God, you're right," she says, shaking her head slowly. "It's...it's just so good to see you again!"

"I was thinking the same thing," I say honestly, "I thought I'd never see you again." And I mean it from the bottom of my heart. I've even forgotten how good it feels to be able to say something so sincere to another human being. I've had to pile on lie after lie for so long to keep my head down and out of trouble with the law that being open with someone feels beyond refreshing.

But I can't be open with her, I suddenly remember, and the glow of joy starts to fade just a bit. I'm still the same man I've created over the past five years. Obviously, I can't let her know any of that. I have to keep myself a secret from her, just like everyone else. I truly didn't think I'd ever see this girl again in my life, and I have been so convinced of that fact that I've never considered what I might do if I found myself in this very situation.

But she's not a girl anymore, she's a woman, just like I'm not a boy anymore, but a man.

We used to be lovers, but we didn't break up. Her parents took her away from me-- far away. So far that I couldn't find her. It was a dark time in my life, and I've always assumed it was a dark one in hers, too. The way she's looking at me right now sure makes me think she never wanted to leave in the first place.

We obviously can't just pick up where we left off...but I have a feeling both of us want to find out how close we can get to that. Just how measured of a chance can I take with her?

"Where do we even start?" she says, asking the very question burning on my mind.

"How about 'how have you been'?"

"That works," she laughs, "I knew I liked you for a reason." She winks, and I can't get over how much it really does feel like we're five years younger again. She jokes and talks the same way she did back then. "I've been pretty good, all things considered. Ever since I had Flora over there," she says, nodding to the child, "I moved out and started kind of chasing my dreams, as whimsical as that sounds to say out loud," she says, blushing and laughing at herself. Meanwhile, my heart is doing flips.

So, the kid is hers, after all? As she glances to the bar, my eyes flit to her hands to look for a wedding or engagement ring, but I see neither. Could she really be single after all these years?

"That sounds amazing, actually," I say with another genuine smile. "You look like it's been going well for you."

"It's...going," she says, and she starts twirling a lock of hair around a finger, then back again. "I'm working as a barista part-time, but...okay, promise you won't laugh."

"We've been laughing this whole time, so no promises," I say with a wink.

"Fair enough," she giggles. "Do you follow podcasts at all?" she asks.

"Not really, but I've heard of a few."

"So, they're kind of like radio talk shows," she explains, "but they're on the internet, and they're usually about a single subject. So, there are cooking podcasts, or travel podcasts, or comedy podcasts, you get the idea."

"So, what's yours about?" I ask, smiling.

"True crime!" she chirps proudly, and for the first time in years, I have to put some effort into keeping a straight face.

"Really?" I say, leaning forward and arching a brow, smiling. "That's fascinating. What does all that entail?"

"Well, I'm trying to break into journalism," she explains.

"Right, I remember you talking about that so much," I say, and she looks touched that I remember.

"For the most part, I just work off what I can find on the internet, but some of my leads let me do some freelance investigative journalism. Since I'd only have to be somewhere physically part-time, I could take little road trips every blue moon to track down a lead-- which is what brings me to Ithaca, incidentally."

If I had to fight to keep a straight face before, it's a real battle now. There's no way...could she really be following up on a tip about a murder I committed? I want to pry for more answers, but just as I open my mouth, Sage and Flora arrive with all our drinks.

"One cherry mocha for you," Sage says to Blossom, setting her cup in front of her, "one nasty black sludge for you," she says to me with a wink, handing me my black coffee, "and some concentrated nasty black sludge for me," she finishes, sitting down with a cup of what appears to be just a double-shot of espresso.

"I got a cookie," Flora says proudly to Blossom, who takes the girl in her arms and sits her on her lap, kissing her on the head.

"Thanks, Sage," Blossom says. "Good timing, you missed all the boring stuff."

"Oh, is she telling you how she's been chasing serial killers around everywhere?" Sage asks, and while we chuckle, Blossom blushes furiously and rolls her eyes.

"What about you?" she asks me, eager to change the subject. "What have you been up to?"

"Nothing half as interesting," I say modestly. I hate feeling like I have to hold back so much from her, but it's necessary.

No matter what I feel for Blossom, and no matter what she might feel for me, I can't let old feelings get stirred up again. My life has no room for that, and more importantly, her life is clearly full and rich. It warms my heart to see her there, with a good relationship between her daughter and sister, thriving and following what she has always wanted to do...but I have to keep it at that. I have to stay back and watch from afar, if anything.

"It can't be too boring if it's enough to get us to run into each other again," she says, and I can't help but smile.

"I'm a consultant for hunters," I explain, and Sage raises an eyebrow.

"That sounds fake. Especially considering your name," she says, and I chuckle.

"It should be. In short, I meet with hunting clubs or, more often, wealthy people who are thinking about buying up woodland to use as hunting grounds. I organize a few meetings between us and some rangers and other wildlife specialists, and I help them make plans for land that ensures the hunting is sustainable and healthy for the environment."

Both Blossom and Sage look mildly impressed, but it's the same rehearsed line I rattle off to my prospective clients. I want to say that really, I'm just a scout for rich people with nothing better to do with their money. But I don't want to show too much sincerity.

Just keep holding back.

"That's awesome," Blossom says, and I can tell she really means it, despite my best efforts. "Sage, that sounds like something you'd be into."

"Does it get you outdoors a lot?" Sage asks.

"Almost constantly," I say, looking down at my strong, rough hands and chuckling. "Takes me all over the northeast. I never thought I'd be doing anything like this five years ago, but I don't have many complaints.

The truth is, much like Blossom, that job is just what pays the bills while I carry on what I consider my true calling. It's both serendipity and cruel irony that our passions put me and Blossom on opposite sides of the fence.

"So, is that what brings you to Ithaca?" Blossom asks.

"Yes," I lie. "But I don't think the appointment that brought me to Ithaca is going to get me anywhere. You'd be surprised how often it happens. Some trust fund baby realizes how much work actually goes into setting up a hunting camp, and suddenly they lose interest and decide to just sign up for a country club."

"Sounds about right," Blossom laughs. "So, you're not living around here?"

"No, I'll be heading back up to Maine soon," I say, shaking my head. "Nothing like a seven-hour drive to the coast to look forward to, you know? But hey, maybe I can get the name of that podcast of yours to keep me company while I drive."

Blossom looks delighted, but she restrains herself, biting her lip for a moment.

"Well, it doesn't actually exist yet, I'm kind of...doing some groundwork to get that started. How soon are you leaving?" she asks suddenly. I can tell what she's angling for, and my heart races. She wants to stay longer and catch up. This whole time, the more responsible part of me has been saying that I need to keep this to nothing more than ships passing in the night, a brief reunion to remind me what I'm fighting for and then we move on with our lives.

But that's not enough for Blossom.

And now that she has brought it up, I know that deep down in my heart, I can't deny her anything. I want it just as bad as she does.

"Long enough to stick around, if you all are going to be here a while," I say.

She smiles at me, then gives her head a little shake, as if snapping herself out of something.

"What's the matter?"

"Nothing, I just..." she trails off, looking into her coffee before looking back up at me with a face that would make an angel jealous. "You remember those white lilac trees we used to sit under, talking about everything until it was too dark to see?"

My heart thuds hard against my chest. Why would she bring that up now, after all this time?

"Of course I do," I say, and she looks delighted.

"I just kind of miss that," she says with a dreamy look on her face, and it's infectious.

"Yeah," I admit, a little relieved for the time being. "Me too."

I am still in shock. It feels like the moment we reached Ithaca, I stepped through some metaphysical veil and ended up in a dream scape. There is no way this is my reality. There is no way I'm actually, truly, legitimately in the same city as the man I lost years and years ago. I had long since given up on my pipe dream of finding Hunter again. It seemed so impossible. I mean, obviously when I was first dragged away from northern Maine and sent away as punishment for my misbehaving ways, I used to fantasize about Hunter showing up out of the fog. I would lie in bed and stare out the window, imagining what it would feel like to see a rock pelting against the pane. I thought I would get up out of bed in my long, white nightgown and check the window to see the boy of my dreams climbing up to rescue me from my tower, like I was some modern-day Rapunzel. But the months had gone by without word or sight of the father of my child, and over time, my hopes turned to idle fantasy, and from idle fantasy into a discarded dream. That's not to say I didn't still long to have him in my arms again. But I knew better than to put all my hopes into a man who didn't know where I was and had no means of rescuing me. For all intents and purposes, I gave up.

Sometimes I still fantasized about running into him at a coffee shop or the grocery store or something. During the lull hours of the afternoon during my shifts at the Lazy Bean, I would stare at the glass door entrance and picture Hunter striding through them, somehow looking exactly as he did five years ago. He was the hero of my every dream. He was the long-suffering but valiant prince searching high and low for his lost princess. At least, that is the role he's always played in my daydreams.

But to have him here now, in the flesh, looking and sounding just as real as the busy streets of Ithaca all around me-- it's almost too much to handle. I keep fighting the urge to pinch my arm and try to wake myself up. I know how it feels to lose everything in an instant, and I'm quietly terrified that it will happen again. That I'll take my eyes off of him for one second and he will evaporate into the air, never to be seen again except for in my fondest, warmest memories. I keep wanting to reach out and touch him, just to remind myself that he's really here. It's like my brain can't even comprehend reality, not after the five long, lonely years I have spent without him. It's too good to be true. *He's* too good to be true.

Especially because he looks so damn good. He's even taller and much sturdier-looking than he even was back then. When I was eighteen and he was twenty-three, he still had a sort of scrappy, lean, almost hungry look about him. Like he had spent much of his life slightly undernourished and incapable of relaxing. I can still recall so perfectly the sensation of his scratchy, patchy beard against my smooth skin when we kissed under the lilac trees. But now, his beard is lushly filled in and even all around, kept neatly trimmed. His dark hair, once tufty and tousled as though he had perpetual bedhead, is thick and well-kept. Where once he was lean and sharp, now he is bulky and hard. Everything about him speaks to his probably newfound ability to look after himself. He's no longer under the thumb of some disinterested foster guardian. He's free to be his own man, to live the life he wants to live. From the sound of it, he's pretty damn successful. He's pulled his life together and really made something of himself, and it shows. Hunter almost shines with an inner glow that draws me to him like a moth to a flame.

I'm proud of him. And I find myself desperately

wishing to make him proud of me, too. I never want to stop talking and catching up. I never want to let him go. And luckily, he seems to feel the same way.

We end up spending hours and hours at the coffee shop just talking and basking in one another's company. I am eternally thankful to have Sage with me, as she does a great job of keeping Flora entertained and relatively quiet while the grown-ups chat. About an hour and a half in, Sage runs out to the car and comes back with a coloring book and a small pack of crayons packed for the express purpose of keeping wandering little hands occupied. And when the morning shifts into afternoon, I notice the barista glancing over at us now and again with a nervous, furtive look that is all too familiar to me.

I lean in closely to whisper to Sage and Hunter, "I think we might had overstayed our welcome here. The barista keeps glancing over at us."

Sage nods. "Yeah, that's true. We have been hogging the table for awhile now."

"Should I buy us another round of coffee to pacify the staff?" Hunter asks helpfully.

I smile. "If I have any more caffeine I might give myself the shakes."

"Fair enough. I forget you're not as hopelessly addicted to coffee as I am. Barely even affects me anymore," Sage says with a shrug.

"Well, when you spend the majority of your

waking hours surrounded by coffee at work, it tends to lose some of its appeal," I chuckle.

"So, where should we go? Or do you need to get going? I'm not holding you up, am I?" Hunter asks, looking back and forth between Sage and me.

I shake my head vehemently, my eyes going wide. I can barely contain my enthusiasm as I jump to assure him we don't need to break apart just yet. "No, no. I don't want to leave yet-- or, well, I mean I don't want to leave you yet. We could always go somewhere else, though," I explain, embarrassed at how over-eager (read: desperate) I sound. I don't dare make eye contact with Sage right now. I can feel her smirking at me. She knows me better than anyone.

Hunter nods and smiles. I think I can detect a hint of relief, as though he's pleased to hear that I want to spend more time with him. As if there would ever be any question about that. Flora, however, is getting impatient. It's easy enough for three adults to sit in one place and chat for hours on end, but for a five year old, it's akin to torture.

"I bored!" she exclaims, setting down her favorite purple crayon decisively.

"She tends to tell it like it is," I remark to Hunter.

"Yeah, no sugar-coating with this one," adds Sage, laughing.

"How about this," Hunter begins, looking at Flora with a sweet twinkle in his eye. "Would you and your auntie like to go see a movie?" Then, he looks at me and mouths the words, *I'll pay*. I grin as Flora starts excitedly bouncing up and down.

"Movie!" she bursts out, clapping. Sage smiles.

"Sounds like a yes to me," she says. "You two should go somewhere and chat, and I'll go see a movie with the little one."

"Are you sure? I don't want to just...abandon you and Flora," I tell her, biting my lip. Secretly, though, I can't wait for it to be just Hunter and me. Don't get me wrong, I love spending time with my sister and daughter, of course, but this could be a once-in-a-lifetime chance to reconnect with the literal man of my dreams. I'll do anything to keep this ball rolling.

"Yeah! Of course. I'd love to," Sage assures me.

"Great!" says Hunter. And with that, it's settled. The four of us head across town to the movie theater, my car tailing after Hunter's. When we get there, he pays for them to see some kids' film about dogs, and the sets of two part ways. Sage and Flora head in to see the movie while Hunter and I walk around the corner to a hip little restaurant tucked away off the beaten path. Finally, it's just the two of us, and from the moment we sit down, the conversation flows as easy as water pouring down Ithaca Falls. Sparks are flying, and my heart is pounding along like crazy just from being in such close proximity to Hunter. It's wild to think that our connection is just as powerful, if not more, than it was all those years ago in small town Maine. We were just dumb kids back then, essentially, but the electricity between us has never faltered.

The restaurant Hunter picks is nice, but not overly fancy. He has good taste. The waiter comes and pours us a couple glasses of red wine and I giggle a little as I raise the glass to my lips. "Too bad we were never able to go on a proper date like this years ago," I tell him.

Hunter nods, a warm smile on his face. "Yeah, your parents would never have let that happen. Besides, that town didn't have a single restaurant suitable for a date with the most beautiful girl in the world."

I blush and hastily take a gulp of wine to distract myself from the compliment. "Plus, I wasn't able to drink back then. It's crazy to think I was just eighteen," I sigh. "So young and so dumb. And so in love."

"So in love," he repeats softly, shaking his head as those cinnamon-brown eyes gaze into mine. "I'd never seen anyone like you before. Do you remember that first day we met? I was being a delinquent, as usual, stealing produce from that grumpy old farmer."

I laugh. "Yes! You leaped over the fence when I was picking berries. I was so shocked."

"I was, too. I knew I needed to keep running so I wouldn't get caught, but you were just so pretty you stopped me in my tracks," he says. "That blonde hair braided down your back, those bright blue eyes. You looked like an angel. I still remember seeing your shoulders just slightly tinged pink from the sun."

"I helped you hide under the bushes when the farmer came looking for you," I recall aloud wistfully. "I still can't believe he bought my story."

"I can. With a face like yours, you could sell anything. I really felt like you had materialized out of thin air to save my ass," he chuckles. The waiter comes back over and we both order: a steak and fries for Hunter, some random chicken dish for me. I've hardly even glanced at the menu. The food doesn't even register on my radar at the moment, even though I'm definitely hungry. All that matters to me right now is the gorgeous man in front of me. He asks me so many questions about myself and, unlike some people who only ask you questions so they can then talk about themselves, I can tell that he genuinely wants to know. He's curious about me, about the life I've led since we were ripped apart. But one thing he pointedly does not ask about is Flora. I haven't told him she's his child, and he doesn't ask. Not yet, at least.

I decide to steer the conversation back to him. After all, I'm curious, too.

"So, what happened to you after we-- after my parents separated us?" I ask, taking a bite of my chicken. It's pretty damn delicious, but not as delicious as Hunter.

"Well," he begins with a heavy sigh, "I spent a lot of time looking for you. Nobody told me where you went. And as I'm sure you remember, I didn't have a whole lot of friends or allies in that town. My reputation wasn't the cleanest, and your folks made everybody promise to keep quiet about where they took you. I tried to track you down, Blossom. I really tried. But it was like you just disappeared into thin air. I couldn't understand it."

"Have you been there all this time?" I ask, leaning forward with sharpened interest.

He shakes his head. "No. I got into some legal trouble back home-- nothing intriguing, just some dumb bullshit, to be honest. But by then, I was ready to leave anyway. You were the only thing keeping me there, and once you were gone, well, there was no reason for me to stay. So I finally stopped moping around and got myself together. I started my career. It was slow-going at first. I never really had anyone to help me, and I was too stubborn to ask for help, anyway. But after a while it took off, and I've been doing it ever since. I never stopped looking for you, though. Even in the smallest ways. So many times I thought I saw you in a crowd somewhere, only to find out it was a trick of the light or something. I just want you to know, Blossom, that even though I've changed in a lot of ways, my feelings for you remain the same as they ever were."

"I looked for you, too," I murmur sadly. "Everywhere. But I didn't have a lot of freedom back then. Almost none at all, actually. My parents...they were so angry with me for disobeying them. I'm sure you can remember how I used to vent to you all the time about how strict and overbearing they were. Sage and I, we felt like prisoners in our own home most of the time. Sage was braver than me. She used to sneak out our bedroom window at night to meet up with friends. With boys. She's always been able to keep her cool under pressure. But as for me, I was always the perfect child. Quiet. Obedient. Helpful. I spent most of my time helping my mom cook and clean, going to church choir practice. I was a soprano and all that," I add with a sheepish smile.

"I remember," Hunter says, beaming at me. "I was never a church-goer myself, but I snuck into the back pew one Sunday just to hear you sing. I don't know if you saw me there, but it was the time when you got that solo hymn. You were so nervous when you told me about it, I knew I couldn't miss it. So I stood in the back, half-hiding behind that big velvet curtain, and I watched you do that hymn by yourself."

"Did you really?" I gasp, clapping a hand over my mouth as my face blushes bright pink. "I had no idea! The lights were so bright I could hardly see past the front two pews, much less all the way to the back. Oh, I was so nervous and it was so hot in that chapel.

I thought I was going to faint in the middle of my solo."

"But you didn't. You were beautiful. You were perfect, Blossom. I remember thinking to myself, 'Wow, not only does she look like an angel but she sounds like one, too,'" Hunter tells me softly. "I knew I was in love with you. I'd never been in love before, and I never thought it would happen to me, but damn. It happened. *You* happened."

As I sit here staring at his handsome, adoring face in the mood lighting, I think to myself that it's impossible. It's impossible that this man, my white-lilac prince, could have anything to do with the murder in Ithaca. It's absurd to even consider it. All of this, every bit and piece, is one huge, beautiful coincidence. Fate brought me here. I thought it was to kick-start my podcast, but really, it was to bring me back to Hunter.

"So, if you're living in Albany, then what brings you here to Ithaca?" he asks. I detect some slight suspicion in his voice, but I dismiss it. Surely, that's not accurate. What reason would he have to suspect my intentions?

"Well," I begin, "I'm kind of here to do some light crime reporting. You know, about that murder that happened here recently. I know I'm just some starry-eyed civilian, but I wanted a chance to get my feet wet. Feel it out. Maybe take some photos and inspire myself to finally start up that podcast. I don't know how yet, but I want to be the one to break this case wide open. I know, I know, it's awfully ambitious. But I want to try."

He nods, looking thoughtful for a moment as the first silence of the day settles in between us. It's not an uncomfortable quiet, though. Just an easy, natural comfortable quiet as we eat dinner and sip wine. But then, seemingly out of nowhere, he looks up at me with a meaningful look on his handsome face, and my heart skips a beat. I know he's about to say something important, even if I don't know what. I set down my fork and knife and look at him expectantly.

"I'm not sure how to phrase this, Blossom, so I'm just going to come right out and ask you: Flora… is she… is she mine?" Hunter asks in a soft, lowered voice.

I feel butterflies stirring in my chest. There's no sense in dancing around the subject anymore. He's here, I'm here, and I can deny him nothing. So I simply smile warmly, nod, and answer him. "Yes, Hunter. She's your daughter."

HUNTER

I should have known trying to get any sleep tonight was going to be useless. I turn my naked body over in the sheets and try to keep my eyes clenched shut, but my mind keeps racing. I'm past the point of being able to lull myself into a relaxed state. My thoughts run fast and get scattered, so much so that I feel disoriented doing nothing. It's frustrating, and it leaves me tossing and turning with nothing but the sounds of the quiet hooting of owls outside.

Knowing that Blossom is just a few feet away from me in the other room doesn't help.

I had rented a cabin in the woods outside Ithaca when I first got here-- not the same woods as those where I killed my victim, of course. It has two bedrooms, so when I found out that Blossom and the girls have been staying in hotels night to night, how could I not offer them the space? The more time I spend with them, the more I want to get the know them. I want to reconnect with Blossom, even though I know it's the last thing any of us need in our lives.

And I alone know that, which makes it even more painful.

Eventually, I realize that there's no use just thrashing in bed for hours on end. I push the sheets off me and swing my thick legs out of bed, standing up and pulling on a pair of comfortable pants and a shirt to pull over my muscles. I open the door so quietly that it's almost soundless, and I slowly make my way out to the porch, being just as quiet.

Outside, I'm treated to a beautiful view of Cayuga Lake. The porch is just a few feet from the water's edge, and a full moon basks the glimmering waters in a trail of silver light leading northward. The moment I'm outside in the cool air, I feel a sense of calm come over me.

It's strange, this isn't the kind of environment where I thought I'd feel at home. In some ways, it's troubling. The stillness and dark beauty of the night draws me in and captivates me, and I know that when I move through the world in these late hours, I'm invincible. This is when I operate, and this is where I hunt.

But being so close to Blossom again after so many years is like being close to my old self. I'm feeling things I haven't felt in five years, and the boy I was back then doesn't feel comfortable shoulder-to-shoulder with the man I am now. On bare feet, I stride to the edge of the porch and slowly sit down, letting my legs hang off the edge as I stare out onto the waters. Every now and then, I see a fish jump. Off in the far distance, I can see a deer cautiously stepping out and looking around before taking a drink from the icy waters.

I hear another hoot from an owl. In the bottom of my heart, I know I have more in common with that owl than any majestic prey of the woods like the deer or the fish. It's a lonely feeling I have a hard time confronting, if I'm honest.

I helped bring a child into the world.

The thought makes my mind go still for several long moments as I stare out onto the waters. It's the first time I've let it really cross my mind since Blossom told me. Shortly after Blossom answered my question, she got a call from Sage, letting us know the movie was over and Flora was eager to see her mommy. There was something touching about listening to that conversation that was only made more meaningful by the news I'd just gotten. I sat there stunned for longer than I realized. What else could I do? We left in a hurry to go collect them, and we haven't had a chance to speak since then.

I grip the wooden planks with my strong hands,

giving them a squeeze, and my thoughts start to come to me one by one.

Could these killer's hands hold a child?

I start to feel the weight of my actions on my shoulders and my conscience. I know for a fact that many of the men I've killed have themselves been parents. Does that make things better or worse? Every person I've killed has been scum. The abusive bastard I killed most recently was no exception. I remind myself that I've never doubted that the world is a better place without the people I remove from it. But that doesn't make the act of killing less meaningful.

Over time, I came to think of myself as a predator in the same way the owl is. It doesn't think about right and wrong, doesn't get burdened by the guilt of snatching mice and fish from their families. It acts according to its nature. That's what I do.

That's what I tell myself, at least. But now that there's a child involved…

For the past few moments, I have felt someone's eyes watching me, and the sound of the creaking screen door confirms my suspicions. The soft footsteps I hear coming toward me are heavier than Flora's would be.

"How long have you been watching me?" I ask Blossom mildly as she appears at my side, slowly sitting down next to me and letting her nearly-bare legs dangle beside mine. I turn to look at her, and my heart skips a beat. Her makeup is off, her hair is loose, and she's wearing just an oversized gray t-shirt and black shorts.

"Long enough to know you've gotten a lot more pensive over the years," she says, smiling. "Can't sleep either, huh?"

"No," I say, chuckling, and I put my hands on the porch to prop myself up as I lean back. "You sound about as surprised as I am."

"I'm sorry we had to run so soon after...after dropping a bombshell like that," she says in a low tone. But I shake my head, dismissing her worries.

"No, don't worry about that. It gave me some time to think about it."

"And what do you think about it?" she asks. I turn to look at her face, and I see her blue eyes shimmering in the moonlight. She looks downright ethereal. I want to grab her and kiss her, push her down onto the porch floor and feel her in all the ways I've craved over the years.

But I can't. For so many reasons, I can't.

"I don't know," I admit, chuckling at myself, and she smiles.

"That's what I said when I found out I was pregnant," she says. Those words hit me like an arrow to the heart.

"I wish I could have been there for you." I take her hand in mine as the honest words spill out of my mouth in a thick, husky tone. "If I'd had any idea…"

"There was no way you could have known," she says, shaking her head and giving me a loving, forgiving smile. That doesn't help the burden I feel, but it's nice to know she doesn't blame me. I'm slient for a few moments before speaking again.

"What happened?" I ask at last. "When you left, I mean."

"I didn't leave," she says quietly, turning to stare out at the lake. The deer at the far end has run off, leaving an empty field of water for us to stare at vacantly. "They took me."

"Your parents?"

"Yeah. You know what they're like."

I frown, furrowing my brow and feeling anger rise up in my heart. Blossom's parents are easily the most controlling people I've ever known. My own parents were as neglectful as they were abusive, but Blossom dealt with a completely different kind of controlling parents. They did everything they could to keep us apart, and they made it very clear that even when she became an adult, they weren't ready to let her out of their claws.

"I always wondered if they were part of it," I say ruefully.

"They weren't just a part of it, they were *all* of it," she says, running a hand through her hair. "As soon as they found out I was pregnant, they knew it was yours. They dragged Sage and me to Albany with them pretty much immediately. Dad already had a job offer on the table he was planning to turn down, but I guess this was just what he needed to give him a push," she adds with a scowl as she stares out at the water. I shake my head.

"What a bastard." I pause for a few long moments, looking down at the water. "Thanks for letting me know. It's fucked up to say, but I think part of me hoped it was like that. Not the fact that it happened, but the fact that it was your parents' decision. But when I didn't hear anything for so long…"

"I had no way to reach out to you, Hunter," she says, turning to me and locking gazes with me, making me look into those pleading eyes. "Don't you think I would have if I had half a chance? I desperately wanted to get a letter out to you, a text, a call, anything. But they put me in one of those…those nunnery places, a big compound where they put 'problem girls' who are pregnant and unmarried. I was in there with a bunch of other girls whose parents were ashamed of them, and the nuns handled all our mail. Nothing got past them. Some of the girls and I even had a deal with one of the delivery men to smuggle some mail out, but he got caught at the last minute."

She falls silent, and I realize there are tears in her eyes. I reach for her face and gently wipe it away, and she looks at me.

"I'm sorry you had to go through that at all, much less alone," I say.

"I had Sage," she said, sniffing. "Sort of. She came to visit as much as my parents would let her. And she was always pushing for it. That meant a lot to me. But by the time they let her come see me without them being there so I could beg her to write to you, you must have moved. She said her letters got returned."

"When I thought you were gone forever, I moved up to Maine to find work," I explain, feeling my heart sink. "I had to. Job opportunities in Albany were…"

"You don't have to explain yourself to me, Hunter," she says, almost laughing, and when I look at her, I see that she's smiling wistfully. "Life tore us apart, plain and simple. We're not the only people that's happened to."

"That doesn't mean we can be okay with it," I say.

"Not okay with it, no," she agrees, and she strokes my hand with her thumb, looking at how well it fits in my bigger one. "But at peace with it, maybe. I don't know. I…I've given it a lot of thought, but Flora made all the difference."

I smile, and I feel warmth all over my body. It's silly, but knowing that Flora was a source of comfort rather than pain felt very good to me.

"It was like having a piece of you with me, in some ways," she says. "Not entirely, of course. She's her own person. She had a personality even she was a baby," she laughs. "But she looks so much like you,

Hunter. I know you saw that the first time you laid eyes on her."

"I saw it, but I didn't want to let myself think it."

"It's a lot to take in," she says, nodding. "Hell, I had nine whole months to take it in before it happened. I wish I'd been able to give you more of a heads up, but…"

"Don't you blame yourself for anything," I say firmly. "Only you know what's best for you, and you did that."

She smiles at me for a long time before continuing.

"Flora was my rock in more ways than one. As soon as she was born, I just left. My parents couldn't legally stop me, all they could do was try to cut off my exit. But I was good at keeping my intentions hidden. Played good girl for a hot minute, then changed bank accounts, got a burner phone, and moved across the city. I would have left the city entirely if I could have, but I wasn't going to leave Sage behind like that."

"Is she with you full-time now?"

She nods.

"As soon as Sage turned eighteen, she moved in with me. Since then, it's been night after night of just gushing about how much hell we went through together. It's been…weirdly therapeutic, actually. For her as well as me."

"That's great," I breathe. "That kind of support is

priceless." I sure as hell wish I had more than just my own thoughts to consume me in the darkest places. Then again, that loneliness is what shaped me into the man I am now.

Is that something to be proud of, or not?

"It really is-- both for her and for me," she says, nodding. "I don't know what I would have done without her."

"She looks up to you," I say. "I can tell. And she's lucky to have such a good role model."

"Yeah, nothing says 'responsibility' like dragging your kid sister and daughter around the state chasing a tip about a serial killer who's still at large."

We laugh, and my heart pounds faster. It's a reminder that every second I spend around Blossom is playing with fire, and this is a fire so hot it could burn us both alive. I couldn't live with myself if that happened. The more time I spend here talking to Blossom, the more I realize what a wonderful person she has become. She's more than just a functional, adjusted adult. She's a woman with hopes and dreams, her feet on the ground, and people who love her. She has everything. To want to step closer into that world is beyond tempting.

But it would destroy her. It would destroy Flora, too.

When we stop laughing, she looks at me with some searching gaze, and I don't resist it at first. But when the silence has gone on too long, she puts both her hands around one of mine and squeezes gently.

"I miss this, Hunter," she says. "I don't know about you, and I guess I made myself forget how much I did, but...I really miss this."

"I do too," I have to admit. I feel her getting closer to me, and I turn to look deep into her eyes. I can feel her pulse racing against my hand. I know the look in those gorgeous eyes so damn well.

Too well.

I want to lean into it. I want to push her back against the deck and feel everything I've craved for years. I want to tell her that she and she alone has been the light keeping me sane and driven for this whole time we've been apart, that she's the reason I can keep on going. I want to spill my heart and tell her how I've never stopped loving her after all these years.

But those can't be the words coming out of my mouth.

"Blossom," I say, covering her hands with my other one, "I'm a different man than I was back then."

"And I'm a different woman," she says, not missing a beat. Her mind is quick as it is beautiful.

"But I recognize her," I say in a low, husky tone, and I bring my hand to her chin, holding her and boring into her eyes with mine. "I've changed in ways you could never know, Blossom. Ways that would frighten you. In my line of work, I've had to do some things that I'm not proud of. I've had to go to some dark places I couldn't ask anyone to follow me through, much less you."

The look she gives me is so attentive, so knowing, that I feel like I'm standing before an angel and having my soul judged when she says the next sentence.

"I know you'd never do anything without a good reason," she says. My pulse races. If only she knew what she was saying.

Or maybe she does? Those eyes are almost haunting. She's insightful, possibly more so than I ever guessed.

The lilac tree...

...does she know?

There is some kind of unspoken question suspended in the air between the two of us. Hunter is looking at me with those dark eyes the color of wood smoke, the color of cloves, with a deep burning fire crackling in the shadows there. I can feel him watching me with the intensity of a fox stalking a rabbit through the underbrush. Like he is a predator I should fear. Like I'm exactly the flavor of prey he most desires, and at any moment, he could spring into action and catch me in his gnashing jaws.

All around us, the forest thrums with nocturnal life. Owls hooting in the distance, rustlings in the trees and brush. And beyond that, the far-off, chilling howl of a wolf echoing in such a way that makes me wonder if it's merely an echo, or just the identical replies of its pack as they wind through the wilderness. This cabin is lodged in the middle of nowhere, essentially. If someone wanted to lure me out to a violent, secret death between the pines where nobody could hear me cry out for help-- this would be the exact sort of real estate at the top of the list.

As soon as that idea occurs to me, I feel a prickle of unease. The first and only little alarm bell dinging in the back of my mind, crying out to my brain that maybe this was a foolish idea to follow Hunter out into the woods. Into his own comfort zone. This is his territory, not mine. Even though I used to live in rural northern Maine, surrounded by rolling fields, rocky shores, and lonely forests, that was a long time ago. Five years. And those five years were not empty, simple ones. They seem like an eternity when I reflect upon them now. Like they expanded wider and wider to contain multitudes of turning points and milestones, all whisked far, far away from the whispers of the woods at nighttime. Five years spent in varying levels of solitude, isolated in a slow-moving cell in the middle of the city.

Perhaps my sister is right. Perhaps I *am* naive. For even though I have grown up, had a daughter, gotten a job, escaped my parents' stranglehold, and become a mostly-independent, self-sufficient woman of the city, I still have so many weak points. There are so many ways to trap me, to lure me away from safety.

Hunter is the lure. My honey-sweet memories of berry-stained kisses under the white lilac branches have carried me out of the safety of my apartment in Albany and floated me all the way here to Ithaca, and now to the hunter's cabin in the woods. Because I know now that I can no longer ignore the twinge of paranoia muffled underneath my joy and surprise at seeing Hunter again. I can't keep lying to myself about why I'm here. Sure, it has something to do with that horrific murder and my podcast dream and my desire to become a crime reporter. But it's much more than that. It's a deeper, more instinctual drive that has brought me three hours from home.

Those white lilacs. I can no longer brush them away as part of the great cosmic coincidence that brought me back to the man I love. The man whose past five years are still partially obscured by mystery. He gave me no minute details. No names. No precise locations. He's never mentioned a permanent home or address. Hunter has a job that keeps him traveling, keeps him on the road all the time, bumping from one neck of the woods to the next. I have listened to so many true crime podcasts. I have stayed up late, rocking my daughter to sleep by the dim light of a table lamp while my free hand scrolls through article after article about unsolved murders and mysteries. I've read hundreds of pages about the psychology behind most serial killers. I've seen pictures of crime scenes. I've read police reports, listened to 9-1-1 call recordings. I have delved into the kind of bloody, bone-chilling world of nightmares that people like my sister would be disgusted by. I know the tricks these killers keep safely tucked up their sleeves. They leave tracks sometimes, whether on purpose to taunt the public and the police or by accident. They leave calling-cards.

White lilacs.

The pure white blooms at the crosshairs, at the intersection of Hunter's life and mine, the flowers that brought us together. By chance? Maybe. Still, I may be naive, but even I have lived enough of life to know that coincidences this huge don't come along very often.

There is a question hanging from my lips, dangling in the air between us, but I cannot seem to give it breath. Because I know that if I do, it will irrevocably change things between us. If I dare to ask this deadly question, there's no telling how far down this crevasse Hunter and I might fall together. And I have to ask myself something else first.

Do I really want to know?

But before I can waver in either direction, Hunter swoops in to swallow up the question with a passionate kiss. It's the kind of kiss with a weight to it. In this case, five heavy years of forced separation, of life changes big and small, of clinging to empty hopes and broken promises. Five years of self-induced isolation and loneliness. I've never taken another lover. Not since I lost the only one that ever mattered to me. Because I still held hope that I'd see him again, and because I knew that even if our paths were never to cross again, I would never, ever find another man I wanted so badly as I want Hunter. At the tender, foolish age of eighteen I made my choice: to fall for and follow this man, with all his darkness and his secrets, hopelessly in love to the very end, wherever and whenever it may come. And judging by the passion, the near-desperation in the way he kisses me, I have a feeling his five years have been spent in a similar fashion. He has walked alone, waiting for me. And suddenly, for the moment, it doesn't matter much to me what he's been doing during all this time. It doesn't matter who he's been with, if anyone.

It doesn't even matter to me what he's done or who he's done it to.

Right now, I am his angel, and he is my prince, and come what may, this is what I want.

So I lean into the kiss, parting my lips ever so slightly as his hands slide up to cup my face. His thumbs trace over my rounded cheekbones, follow along my jawline, and back to lightly stroke my hair, pushing the loose locks of blonde hair back behind my ears. We have no need for words right now. We might as well be under those lilacs again, only five years older and five years more desperate for touch. His tongue gently probes into my mouth and I allow it, our lips moving together softly at first, then harder. My entire body is warming up from my toes to the top of my head. I can feel that aching between my thighs, my arms hooking around him as his hands rove down my frame. I've grown up a little since we were last together, and I feel him groan appreciatively as his hands cup my much-fuller breasts. He gropes them hungrily, his fingers dancing over my nipples, squeezing and rolling them between his fingers through the thin fabric of my oversized night shirt. I press myself harder into his hands, sighing as he breaks our kiss and begins to lightly nip at my neck. I'm just as ticklish there as I always was, and with every gentle bite and kiss, I shiver and moan, getting slick between my legs in anticipation.

Hunter pushes my long blonde hair over one shoulder to free up the other, and he tugs the loose-fitting shirt over my shoulder to expose my collar-bone. He leans in and kisses it while his hands play with my breasts, squeezing and feeling them up like we're still two innocent lovers in in the moonlit fields. He moves his way down slowly, one hand sliding around to grab my ass while the other roves down my front. He kisses my lips again softly while his hand travels down between my thighs, and I inhale sharply, surprised and turned on by his forwardness.

"You don't waste any time at all, do you?" I whisper breathlessly.

"I think five years is long enough to wait," he growls in reply.

I can't argue with that. I'm not wearing any panties under my black pajama shorts, and when he tugs them to one side, his fingertips just barely brush along my slick folds, making me tremble and whimper. I want more. I need more.

"I never thought I would get to feel you again like this," Hunter murmurs, slipping his fingers underneath my shorts and lightly stroking up and down my opening.

I'm panting heavily, both arms outstretched so that my hands can brace myself against the wooden wall of the deck. I'm leaning back as he bends down, getting a better angle to slowly slide two long, thick fingers inside my dripping cunny. My hips buck involuntarily as my head falls back and I choke out his name. "Hunter!"

"So wet for me, just like you always were," he murmurs. His fingers push all the way inside of me to brush against my g-spot, making me shiver and grip the wooden posts so hard I might get splinters. As his fingers slide in and out of me, Hunter looks up at me with lidded eyes, his lips parted as though he's just dying to taste me.

"I-I haven't even-- been touching myself-- all

these years," I breathe, "because I knew it would never-- feel as good-- as the way you touch me."

"Fuck, you have no idea how sexy you are, Blossom," he growls, shaking his head. "I've been dreaming about touching you like this for five long years. Five *hard* years."

While his two fingers slip in and out of my aching hole, his thumb starts to gently circle my clit. It's such an overwhelming sensation that I have to gasp for breath and hold on tight. My legs are shaking, and I don't know how much longer I'll be able to hold myself up. Luckily, Hunter seems to notice how much I'm struggling, and he kneels down in front of me, tugging down my shorts and tossing them aside before hooking my left leg up over his shoulder. He wraps a strong, powerful arms around my right leg, keeping me steady while he leans in. Hunter pushes up my gray night shirt and I grab hold of it, bunching it up over my taut stomach to keep it out of the way. I look down at him, my chest heaving as I fight to keep breathing. I'm so overwhelmed and shocked by what's happening that it hardly feels real.

Hunter is here, and he's touching me. He's leaning in, pushing three fingers inside of my pussy now. I'm so slick, I can feel my honey dripping down his arm onto the wooden deck. And when he dives in to start suckling at my clit, I cry out, convulsing with pleasure. I tremble and moan, nearly losing my grip on the wooden post, but Hunter holds me up with his strong arms. And he doesn't let up for a second. I can feel his appreciative moan vibrating up through my pelvis as he devours my pussy, licking and sucking my clit while his fingers pump into my tight, clenching hole. He eats my pussy like it's the most delicious thing he's ever tasted, like he can hardly stand to take a moment to breathe before diving back in.

We've wanted this for so long. Both of us. With every move he makes, with every sigh that falls from my lips, it becomes abundantly clear to me that I don't even care what brought us here together tonight. I don't care if it's fate or coincidence or some wild cosmic conspiracy-- as long as I have Hunter touching me, loving me, giving me the satisfaction and wholeness I've been lacking for five years, none of the details matter.

I need him. He needs me. And I intend to do everything in my power to keep us together this time. I won't lose him again. Not if I have anything to do with it.

I'm rocking my hips now, riding against his face and his fingers even though he's the one in control, and I'm getting closer and closer to climax. I can feel it approaching, that pent-up release hurtling toward me like a tornado.

"Oh god," I gasp. "Hunter... I'm so close."

He growls, "Good. Give it to me, angel. I want to taste you."

Hunter's fingers pump into me faster and harder, striking that deep, delicious spot within me every time while his tongue laps at my clit. My whole body is tensing up, preparing for orgasm when suddenly, there is the unmistakable sound of something-- or someone-- moving around inside the cottage. Both of us freeze up instantly. Hunter looks up at me from between my thighs and I stare down at him, biting my lip. We pause for a few moments, listening closely.

It dawns on me that it could be Sage or Flora getting a glass of water or something, but on the off chance that either one of them comes outside to the deck to check on us, the last thing I need is for my sister or my daughter to find me in a compromising position. Without exchanging a single word, Hunter catches on and gets to the same page. He hastily helps me step into my shorts and pull them up before he stands up beside me, tall and steady. I'm a little disappointed to have been interrupted just before I could finish, but I know I have to be careful. Besides, I fully intend on picking up where we left off as soon as an opportunity presents itself.

Hunter turns to me, his lips parting to say something, probably about Sage or Flora, when there's another sound from inside the cottage. And this time, there's no mistaking it for either of the girls. My stomach twists with anxiety and my eyes go wide. Hunter looks toward the cabin with his jaw clenching, and holds an arm out in front of me, as though to keep me back. That tells me he heard the same thing that I heard: heavy footsteps, probably wearing boots. Neither of the girls could sound like that, even if they tried. Hunter reaches into a pocket of his work jacket and pulls out a blade that glints in the moonlight. A hunting knife.

As he stealthily moves toward the door to open it and go investigate, a dark realization passes over me: the Ithaca killer uses a hunting knife.

HUNTER

Every nerve in my body is under my complete control. This is where I thrive-- hunting in the darkness, stalking my prey, striking with quick and deadly precision. But this time, I'm not the true hunter. We're being hunted by someone else, and I'm not about to take that lying down.

As I stalk forward through the house, the knife in my hand may as well be an extension of my arm. Before I started killing, I trained day and night with knives of all lengths and types, and I mastered their use. Whether it's a freshly killed deer or a living man, I know how to handle myself with a knife as easily as a martial artist handles his fists.

I keep a hand back behind me to discourage Blossom from getting too close. I know she won't just stay put like I want her to, not because she's defiant, but because her only child is in this house with whoever is intruding on us. Not even I could practice that kind of self-restraint. I'd already be on top of whoever was in the house. But I have to be cautious as much as I can. One wrong move, and the intruder will get away.

And I'm *very* interested in knowing who's here.

I was supposed to be out of the cabin by tonight. I was supposed to get all my stuff out and be long gone hours ago, but when I first rented the place, the owner told me it didn't really matter, because he was out of town and wouldn't be back for a few more days.

That meant that whoever is here knows my schedule.

No burglar who knows what he's doing breaks into a cabin knowing that nobody's staying there. There's rarely anything worth taking unless they're just looking for a quick smash and grab, in which case he wouldn't show up while our cars are parked outside. But why would he come in anyway after seeing those cars? My mind is racing, and I'm trying to think of who might be hounding me like this. There's no time, though. I have to keep my entire mind focused on being ready for anything.

I step into the living room and can hear rustling in the kitchen. It's soft, like someone searching carefully. But if the intruder is in the kitchen, he can't be looking for valuables, can he? What the hell is this guy's game?

I'm perfectly silent as I stalk forward, listening to the sounds of things getting moved around carefully and only daring to step down on a new board as something else gets moved in the kitchen. Just before I reach the doorway, the sounds stop, and so do I. There's a moment where I feel the entire house go still, and my muscles tense up.

The next second, a figure swings around the corner.

My whole body reacts, moving back to bear the extra weight as I turn and let him come down onto me with full force before stepping aside and letting his weight carry him past me. I hear the sound of a knife slicing through the air where my face had been half a second ago.

As I turn to follow him with my eyes, I drink in the scene all in the blink of an eye.

The moonlight filtering in through the front door gives me a proper look at the burglar. He's a big man, almost enough to rival me, and he's dressed in all black-- a black ski mask, black sweater, black pants, and black boots. More alarmingly, there's also a black combat knife in his hand. His eyes are so wide that I can see the whites of them.

And in the split second before he lunges at me again, I see Blossom standing in the doorway, hands on her mouth as she holds back a scream.

The attacker lunges at me, but this time, he takes advantage of my surprise. I get a hand around his wrist and hold the knife back by sheer strength, but the force of his tackle knocks me to the ground. I take him with me, getting a knee up and into his stomach. We grapple rolling over the floor, but he doesn't say anything. We don't even grunt.

I want to keep quiet so as not to wake the girls. They don't need this kind of trauma. But the stranger is getting more confusing by the moment. He tries to get an arm down to my neck, but I twist out of the way and manage to get a punch to his gut. On the best of days, wrestling with someone on the ground like this is a chaotic mess, even more so when you both have knives out and ready to slice into anything they touch. In the dark, it doesn't matter how much training either of us has-- it's any man's game.

I push forward and get on top of my attacker, and I swing a hard left hook down on him that he barely manages to turn his head in time with. It connects, but not half as hard as the blow I threw. A moment later, I realize I don't have his knife-hand in sight, and I get up off him just half a second before the blade flashes where my kidney would have been.

Without a second thought, I swing my leg out and kick the knife-hand as hard as I can. He grunts in pain, and the knife goes sliding out the door, past Blossom. My heart jumps to my throat, but she jumps back as fast as if a rattlesnake had slithered out in front of her. In the blink of an eye, the attacker wrenches free and barrels out the door. I'm not about to let him get away this easily, though.

I take off after him, and when I see him reaching for the knife, I jump up and let my body weight carry me into him at full force, feet first. He turns just in time to brace himself, saving him some broken bones, but our bodies crash together and go rolling off the porch onto the banks of the lake.

Wet sand and pebbles crunch under us as we hit the ground. The second we're down, I bring my knife down on him, but he rolls out of the way, and I sink the blade into cold earth. He swings a punch at me, but I bring the knife up in an arc as I twist away.

This time, I feel it connect.

It drags across his bicep, and some of the sweater tears away like paper. I see red blood flow from the wound, but he doesn't so much as wince. Adrenaline is pumping through his veins just like it's coursing through mine. But I don't just see bare skin around the wound. There's something else-- tattoo ink?

I only see it for a moment before he lunges at me again. But now that I've had a moment to get my bearings, I'm more than ready for him. He evades my knife, but I roll into his tackle and swing him under me, using his own body weight to drive him into the ground, landing my knee squarely below his ribcage and knocking the wind out of him. His arms hit the ground on either side of him.

I bring my knife to his throat in less than a

second, pressing it against the fabric where his ski mask meets his sweater. If this were any other night, the blade would already be across his throat and letting blood spill out over the pebbly soil…

But I hear Blossom's panicked gasp behind me, and I freeze, looking into the bastard's eyes.

If I kill him now, in front of Blossom, it will scar her forever. Not only that, but she'll know full well what I'm capable of. She has a damn quick mind, too-- there's a good chance she could figure out what I really am.

I worry that she already suspects me of being the lilac killer.

All this flashes through my mind in half a second, but half a second is all the hesitation my enemy needs. Those eyes see mine, and they know exactly why I haven't killed him yet. That's all he needs to see in order to know I won't kill him tonight.

He wrenches my knife away with one hand, and in that split second, I see the tattoo on his arm-- it's a bird, an eagle with its wings spread out wide and its beak sticking up, open, screaming.

Why does it look familiar?

I don't have any time to contemplate it. The attacker is up on his feet the next moment, but rather than engaging with me, he turns and bolts. The only other man I've seen run as fast as him is myself, and I know that if I ran after him, I might just be able to chase him.

But if I did that, I'd be leaving behind Blossom and the girls. If there are more men like him here tonight, or if he evaded me and doubled back around, I wouldn't be able to live with myself.

I stay put, watching him go as I hear the ringing in my ears.

"Are you okay?"

Blossom's terrified voice snaps me out of my trance, and I turn around to see her staring at me with a sheet-white face and wide eyes. She looks like she's about to faint, so I step forward and hug her with one arm, holding the knife far away from her as I press her against my form. She can't help but let out a single sob before sniffing and forcing herself together, looking up at me. "What the hell was that?"

"Burglar," I say, but I don't think either of us believe that. "Bastard must have thought we're just tourists who would all be asleep tonight."

She nods, but realization hits us both at the same time.

"Flora!" we say as one.

We hurry back into the house and down the hall. Blossom left the door ajar, and I slow to a halt at it, silently pushing the door open. Both our jaws drop.

Flora and Sage are both sleeping peacefully, looking hardly worse for wear. A sliver of moonlight shows me Flora's serene face as her back rises and falls with each breath. As the two of us watch, I feel my heart melting at the sight, and I raise an eyebrow at Blossom.

"Heavy sleepers," she says with an unbelieving smile. "I swear they could sleep through a train wreck."

I roll my eyes and feel laughter in my chest. I can't believe it, either. I just fought off a potentially lethal situation, adrenaline still running hot through my blood, and yet here I am, laughing at a joke Blossom made as if we've been making small talk and flirting all night. It feels good. Damn good.

It makes me feel like we're a family.

My heart beats in my throat, and I look down at the smiling Blossom for a thoughtful moment. I take her hand and lead her back into my room, where I set the knife down on the dresser and pull her in slowly, looking into her wary eyes.

"Hunter, what…?" she trails off, but she can read my intentions in my eyes. I lean forward, bringing my lips to her neck, and I feel the warm skin I've wanted to feel against me for five long, long years. She shivers, but she doesn't pull back. In fact, after a moment, she turns her head, exposing more of her to me as I grip her hips and ravish the side of her neck with kisses, feeling my cock start to harden between my legs.

"Blossom," I growl in a thick, husky voice in her ear. "We need to finish what we started. Now."

BLOSSOM

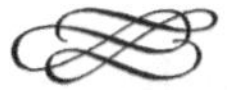

In the dim bedroom, it takes a little while for my eyes to adjust. The thin strains of moonlight filter in through the blinds, casting black and white shafts across the bed, almost like the keys of a piano. Hunter takes my hand and presses it to his heart as he tugs me close, and I know with a wry smile that we are going to make all kinds of beautiful, desperate, passionate music all over those keys. The bed is tousled, sheets pulled all over the place, indicating that even before we talked outside and before that horrible intruder broke into the house, Hunter must have been having one fitful, restless night. I wonder what he was thinking about when he was in bed without me. I wonder what he's thought about every night the past five years, what he's dreamed about. Where has he been? What has he seen?

Who has he been?

I know how silly I am to have ever considered for a split second that the man of my heart and the father of my child could be a killer. Specifically, the same brutal killer who murdered that man in Ithaca. The white lilac was a red herring. It was nothing. Perhaps it wasn't even intentional. Stranger things have happened, that's for sure. Like this, for example: accidentally bumping into the long-lost love of my life in the last place I'd expect to find him. If we had arrived in Ithaca even five minutes later, if we hadn't gotten stuck in traffic on Main Street, if I hadn't just happened to look up and see Hunter crossing the road in front of my car, none of this would have happened. I would have gone on with the rest of my quiet life still totally in the dark, still lonely and lost and longing for the man I could never touch again.

But now he's here, and his hands are on my body. Moving me. Caressing me back to life. And that's the way it truly feels to me. Like I have been wobbling through life on autopilot for the past five years. Of course I have had love all along. I have my sister, Sage, who is whip-smart, dependable, and funny. She's kept me laughing, kept me upbeat through the dark times. And I have Flora, my perfect, innocent little daughter. There's not a single cell of meanness in her body. She's as soft and full of light on the inside as she is on the outside. I've always wondered what it would feel like for Hunter to see her. Would he be proud? Would he be freaked out? I mean, I couldn't blame him if so. It's got to be one hell of a big shock to find out that you've had a secret child all these years. But I saw the look on his face when we peered into their bedroom to see Flora resting her little head on the pillow. I caught the flash of intense wonder and adoration in Hunter's eyes-- the brown eyes so similar to hers.

Surely it is impossible for any man who looks at his daughter that way to be a dangerous man. You can't be both, right? Hunter is just what he says he is. That's what I have to believe. It's ridiculous to think otherwise. Isn't it?

And yet, as his hands slide down my arms to grab my hands and interlock his fingers with mine, I have to wonder: what evil acts have these same hands committed? His touch, so sensuous and loving, so warm and tender, could not possibly be perverted to create pain and torture. I just can't seem to reconcile the two images in my mind, and yet I also cannot extricate myself from the equation. Because I know the truth-- *my* truth. That no matter what he has or has not done, no matter who he truly is and how vastly it differs from the Hunter I loved under the white lilacs, I can never turn away from him. Not now, not ever. I'm in this for however long he'll have me. Even if it's just for the night.

Hunter turns me to face him, those brown eyes

glinting in the low light. He's framed by the window, that rectangle of soft light every now and then brightened by a flash of distant lightning. I can hear the first pitter-patter drops of rain against the wooden deck as he pulls me close. We lean in slowly at first, his hands stroking my arms, calming me the same way he used to years ago, when I came to him upset over something my parents did or said. He was my shelter then, and he is my sanctuary now. I roll up onto my tiptoes to kiss him, and the second his lips brush against mine, I part my mouth to let out a low moan. His hands slide up to cup my breasts gently, flicking and pinching my erect nipples through my t-shirt. I melt into him, letting his tongue explore my mouth while he gropes my breasts, my ass, cups the warm, slick mound between my legs. We were interrupted earlier before I was able to finish, and despite the terror of having an intruder in the house, my arousal never faded for a second. It was simply postponed.

Much like my love and lust for Hunter. Even over the five years we spent apart, my desire for him never wavered. I've been craving him all this time, and I can hardly wait to finally sate my needs. Hunter lifts my shirt up over my head and drops it to the floor, exposing my perky breasts, taut stomach, and arching back. He kneels down to help me peel off my black shorts, then tosses those aside, too. I'm stark naked now, goosebumps rising up on my bare skin in the cool air. I lick my lips, anticipating getting to see more of Hunter, too.

He knows what I want. He stands back and tugs his shirt off over his head, throwing it onto a chair along with his boxer shorts. His massive cock springs free, bouncing slightly and totally erect. I need to taste it, suddenly. More than anything. I give him a questioning look and Hunter nods slightly.

Immediately, I drop to my knees and crawl the few steps closer to him, looking up at his face with wide, innocent eyes. My heart pounding like crazy, I reach up and take his thick, glorious shaft in my hands, reveling in the girth and length. I pump up and down a few times, feeling the silky skin glide under my fingertips. Then I lean in and gently tug the head of his cock into my mouth, moaning at how good it feels to be stretched out this way. My cheeks bulge as I slowly, carefully swallow him down to the root, letting my tongue swath along the sensitive underside and around the tender, engorged head.

"Just like that, Blossom," he groans, pushing softly at the back of my head. I bob up and down on his hard cock, lapping up precome and swirling my hands around his shaft in tandem with my mouth. He tastes salty-sweet and warmly familiar. I suck him down eagerly, kneeling in front of him and looking up at his face to see the expression of twisted pleasure and restraint on his handsome, sharp features. I can feel the hardwood flooring creak and grind against my knees, and I know I'm going to have bruises from this, but I don't care. In fact, I kind of relish the idea of having marks left on my body. Because I don't know how much time Hunter and I have together this go around. Maybe it'll just be tonight. And if so, I'm going to need some small souvenirs for the road. Signs that this really did happen. Bruises, bite marks, anything to remind me for the next few days that I truly did spend a glorious, sexy night with the man I loved and lost. This could be the only chance I get.

So I better damn well make the most of it.

I'm fondling his heavy balls while my lips slide up and down either side of his cock, then tug his head between my lips and flick my tongue around, teasing him just a little before pushing down further. By now, Hunter is starting to lose control, inch by inch. He's groaning and murmuring my name, which makes me feel so powerful it spurs me on even more. I love the feeling of his silky skin, his hard length, twitching and straining in my mouth. My cheeks ache, my mouth is salivating, and all I want is to make him feel amazing. I want to blow his fucking mind, prove to him that even though I've been celibate these five years without him, I've still grown up quite a bit. I'm not the virginal, innocent, shrinking violet I was back then when we rolled around and tangled in each other's arms under the lilac blooms.

We are two grown-ass adults now, and I want him to fuck me like one.

Before I can bring him over the edge, Hunter reaches down to gently nudge me back. His cock springs out of my mouth with a wet pop, which makes me grin mischievously and lick my lips as I look up at him. Hunter takes my chin in his hand and traces his thumb over my swollen bottom lip. I suck his thumb into my mouth and his lips fall open in a soft gasp of appreciation.

"You're dirtier than I remember," he growls, helping me to my feet.

I daintily wipe my mouth and smile, feeling my cheeks flush pink. "A lot can change in five years," I tell him, and when his smirk falters for a moment I rush to assure him, "there's been no one else, Hunter. Nobody but you."

He scoops me up into his arms like I'm some damsel in distress, and leans in to kiss me. I can feel my wetness dripping down my thigh as he carries me to the bed. "Surely you must have gotten lonely from time to time," he says softly. He lays me back on the bed, my head on the pillow. As he bends to kiss me, I respond.

"Of course," I murmur, letting his lips gently brush over mine. "But I knew no one else would compare."

He smirks. "It's been the same for me, Blossom. Ever since I first tasted you years ago, I knew there was no point in searching for a substitute. There is nothing sweeter than you."

Hunter moves between my legs, lowering himself down to kiss the insides of my thighs, making me shiver. I bite my lip as he nuzzles closer to my slick folds, his tongue lightly tasting me, circling my clit in teasing motions. My hands grab fistfuls of the bed sheets as I prepare for the ride of my life. He takes two fingers and slowly, tantalizingly slides them inside me while he eats my pussy. I arch my back and moan, closing my eyes and letting my head fall back. A third finger joins as he licks and sucks my clit, moving faster and deeper with every stroke. It's almost trancelike, how rhythmic and repetitive the movements are. Perfectly in sync, tickling that spot deep inside me while the rigid tip of his tongue grinds against the nub of my clit. I begin to moan incoherently, trying and failing to stifle the noise. I don't want my sister or daughter to hear me, but at the same time, I'm losing control. Hunter moves faster and faster, never breaking rhythm for even a second, until finally I'm on the edge of coming.

"Oh, Hunter," I whimper weakly. My whole body is starting to shake. But before I can reach the brink, he stops. I gasp in confusion and disappointment, my eyes opening to stare at him pleadingly. But there's a devilish look on his face, and I know he stopped for a good reason.

"You're teasing me," I pout.

He straddles me hooking my legs over his shoulders as he bends down to kiss me softly. I can feel the head of his thick cock positioned at my slick opening, and I hold my breath in anticipation. Those dark eyes gaze into mine deeply. "When you come, I want to feel it. I want that sweet honey all over my cock, Blossom. I can't guarantee I'll be gentle. I want you...more than you could ever know, angel," he growls.

Before he does anything else, he reaches out to fumble in the bedside drawer. He takes out a condom, but I push his hand away, biting my lip. Flora is the best thing to ever happen to me. And I can't imagine fucking the father of my child with anything between us.

"I think we're long past that, aren't we, Hunter?" I point out gently.

With a grunt of agreement, he drops the condom and leans to kiss me on the forehead before rearing back. I watch with bated breath as he slowly, gradually slides his thick cock inside my aching cunny. With every centimeter, I tremble and moan. It's almost too much. I thought his fingers felt better than anything in the world, but this? There's nothing that can compare to Hunter's cock stretching out my tight little hole, slipping down so deep as to brush against my g-spot without even trying.

"Fuck, Blossom," he snarls between gritted teeth. "I've missed this."

"Promise me one thing," I murmur breathlessly.

"Anything, angel," Hunter says.

"Promise me...you won't hold back," I beg him.

It's like I've said the magic words, because immediately, Hunter pulls back and spears into me so hard I see stars. I cry out as his cock slides in and out of my twitching pussy, slamming into that delicious place deep within, my own slickness dripping down everywhere. He bends forward, crunching my body so that my ankles are nearly around his neck, he's plunging so deeply into me. It feels like he could touch my cervix, he's pounding so hard and fast. Both of us are panting and groaning, clinging to each other for dear life while we fuck hard, making up for lost time with every powerful thrust. I roll my hips up to meet each stroke, clenching my pussy around his thick shaft, bringing us both closer and closer to orgasm.

"You feel so good, baby," he snarls in my ear. His hot breath tickles my neck and gives me goosebumps, as well as a thrill of pure pleasure that connects down to my pussy. His hand reaches around to smack my ass hard while he fucks me, the two of us moving and gasping like wild animals in heat, like we can't help ourselves. There's no doubt about it now: we're just as desperately hot for each other tonight as we ever were five years ago. In fact, it's almost like the absence has stoked our fire. I would sooner die than slow down now.

"Harder," I breathe. "Make it hurt."

Hunter grunts and picks up the pace, an intense, dark expression on his face as he takes my permission to lose control. He's not holding back. He's done restraining whatever wild demon is inside him, so insatiable for my sweet, tight pussy. Hunter grabs my hips so hard I know it'll leave bruises, and that only turns me on even more as he fucks me wildly. We're so close now, both of us gasping in tandem, and then finally-- we're there.

Just as the most powerful climax rips through my body, Hunter dives forward to capture my cry with a kiss, and his cock pumps hot, precious seed deep inside me, filling me up, making me his own. I belong to him now: mind, body, and soul. I know now that nothing-- not time, not space, not bad luck, not good nor evil can break us apart again. Come what may, I belong with Hunter, and he belongs with me.

We come down from the shared high slowly, breathing heavily and kissing each other's faces as our bodies start to go limp. I ache all over in the best possible way, and I can't wait to examine my bruises and marks later. Hunter collapses down next to me with a sigh, leaning over to kiss me on the cheek sweetly. I smile and nuzzle closer, wanting to stay like this forever. But I've had a child, so my ability to, well, resist the urge to *go* has been significantly decreased. So I settle for a kiss to the tip of Hunter's nose, and then I slide out of bed.

Wrapping a sheet around my body, I tell him quietly, "I'll be back. Bathroom."

Hunter nods sleepily, watching me leave. I shuffle down the hallway as silently as I can, not wanting to wake Sage or Flora on the way. I find the bathroom, a little wood-paneled room with a rain shower and a surprisingly wide window. At first, having lived in the city for years now, the sight of a window in a bathroom makes me uneasy. What if someone could see right in? But then I remind myself that this is the middle of nowhere. All I can see through the thin, lightly fluttering, sheer curtains is a strangely familiar but stationary shape. I'm so intrigued that I go to check the window before even going to pee. I part the curtains ever so slightly to look outside, and when my eyes fall on the familiar form, my heart plummets.

Right outside, in full view of the bathroom window, is a gorgeous white lilac tree, almost glowing under the eerie light of the moon.

"What do you think, chocolate chips or banana?"

Flora stares up at the sizzling pan with a look of deep concentration, and I can't help but smile at her as she focuses on this most pressing decision. She looks like she's about to reply a few times, and my smile grows as I hover my hand over the bananas and the bag of chocolate chips in anticipation. Flora can't seem to decide, though, and she looks up at me with a deeply distressed face.

"I don't know!" she proclaims at last, and I chuckle, crouching down and whispering as if I'm hatching a secret plan with her.

"Here's what we're going to do, then, but don't tell your mom. Promise?" I put a finger to my lips and make a zipping motion for emphasis. Her eyes widen in awe, and she nods quickly, zipping her lips shut too. I stand up and cut the bananas in half, then pour out half the usual serving of chocolate chips into a measuring bowl.

"What are you doing?" she whispers, glancing nervously over her shoulder.

"We're going to add *both!*" I say with a wicked grin, as if revealing a world-shaking secret to her. She looks appropriately shocked and amazed, but she's all too willing to be complicit in this heinous crime. She cranes her neck over the edge of the counter to watch as I add both ingredients to the pancake mix I'm making, and I hear Sage laughing from the living room.

"She's gonna try to hide and find a way to stay behind with you, if you keep that up," Sage jokes while I finish mixing the batter and start pouring pancakes into the hot pan. I grin at the comment and watch the batter spread out into an almost perfect circle.

Blossom is sleeping in this morning. I was up before dawn, as usual, and she didn't seem to wake up when I got out of bed and headed into the kitchen. That was all for the best, because I don't think it's a good time for Sage to know what's going on between me and her big sister. Not that I think she's oblivious enough to have not picked up on it, but now simply isn't the time to have that kind of conversation.

It also gives me a little quality time with Flora, which I wasn't expecting to ask. I was staring out over the lake with a mug of black coffee in my hand when she crept out to see me, and from the moment she groggily asked if we were going to have breakfast this morning, my heart was sold. The kid could probably ask me to buy this cabin and I'd do it.

"Okay," I tell Flora, "this is the delicate part. Everyone knows the first pancake is always a mess. It never comes out right. Do you want to help me try to flip it?"

She worries her lip, looking anxious, glancing between me and the griddle.

"I don't know if I reach…" she says at last, embarrassed. I give a hearty laugh, and a moment later, I've scooped her up into my arms. She gives a squeal of delight, and I hold her up so that she's facing the pan, well away from the hot metal. I hand her the spatula and get her to grip it with both of her small hands. It's easy enough to do, since she weighs nothing and rests easily in one of my arms.

"Hold it carefully," I say, "and you'll want to slide the edge under the pancake all the way. Then just pick it up and tilt it to the side, fast. And remember, it's completely okay if it folds over or falls out of the pan. We have plenty of batter."

She nods as if accepting a sacred mission, and she prods at the side of the pancake cautiously. If she leaves it much longer, it'll burn, but I don't want to hurry her too much and confuse her. But to my surprise, she slides the spatula underneath the pancake like a pro, heroically lifts it up with a panicked face, and turns it sideways.

It hits the pan with the skill of a trained chef, and it gives a satisfying sizzle. Flora and I both stare at it with stunned faces for a moment.

"You did it!" I cheer triumphantly, lifting her up in the air and tossing her up, catching her as she giggles gleefully. She also drops the spatula during this move, but my reflexes are good enough that I catch it with ease.

"Yay!" she cheers with me, and I tend the pancake with her in my arms until it's cooked to perfection.

"What about you, Sage?" I call into the living room.

"Uh...what about me?" she asks in almost a scoffing tone. I get the feeling that teenage moodiness hasn't totally left her yet, which I can't blame her for one bit.

"Chocolate, banana, or both?"

She pauses, seeming kind of surprised that I offered, but finally, she gives a curt answer from the living room.

"...chocolate. Bananas give me weird hives."

"Roger that," I say.

Flora and I make a whole heaping plate of pancakes, with her proudly flipping each one until she has the art down to perfection. Once enough are made for the rest of us, I quickly clean the pan to scrub off the banana residue and whip up a few more quick ones with just chocolate. The cabin owner keeps this place well stocked, since he seems like he's used to families and long-term vacationers staying here. After about ten minutes, the three of us head outside to the porch to sit on the wooden planks and dig into our food while watching the lake.

"You're an amazing chef, you know?" I tell Flora as she scarfs down her second pancake with the ferocity of a teenager. She beams at me through a mouth full of food, and I chuckle. "I could see you as a star chef someday, if you stick to it."

"Yeah!" she says enthusiastically, turning to Sage with stars in her eyes. "Sage, will Mommy let me be chef?"

"Mommy would let you be anything you want to be," Sage laughs through a bite of her own food.

As I beam down at Flora, I can't help but feel how idyllic this all is. Flora doesn't know who I am to her, and she doesn't need to know right now, but sitting here and getting along with the family makes me feel like I've been a part of it all along. I don't know how to explain it, but it feels like a piece of a puzzle fitting into place after being gone too long. I'm even more surprised that I like the feeling. It makes me feel warm and complete in a new way I never knew I was missing.

Finally, I look over to Sage, who has been understandably quiet for all this. The last time I saw her, she was about fourteen. A lot must have changed over the years, and I don't know what she thinks about me yet. I can't deny what I feel for Blossom, and that should be enough, but now that I'm spending time with the whole group of them, I start to wonder how they feel about their caretaker having feelings for someone.

"Blossom and I talked a little about the past few years," I say to her in a somewhat more serious tone as Flora gets engrossed in her food. "It sounds like things have been hard."

Sage chuckles ruefully at that.

"You have no idea." She nods to Flora, then looks to me. "But that kid right there is the glue that kept us together, believe it or not. When they had Blossom...hidden away," she says in a low tone, obviously trying to hide some of the trauma from Flora herself, "it was bad. Real bad."

"Yeah?"

"They hounded me after what happened with Blossom. Figured I wasn't far off from running away and doing the same thing, you know? I mean, they were right, because I did try to run away more than once."

"You're kidding," I say, though in truth, I'm

completely unsurprised. Sage has a kind of fighting spirit to her that has always been there.

"Farthest I ever made it was a gas station halfway down to NYC where the cops picked me up," she says with a sigh. "Sometimes I wonder what things would have been like if they hadn't gotten to me. I had a friend of a friend who had a couch for me to crash on. I'd probably have ended up on the streets, knowing those people, but at the time, even that sounded better than what I was dealing with at home. I know it sounds like stupid teen sh… stuff," she stops herself from swearing, glancing at Flora. "But the thought process is like, if I stayed home, I knew for a fact things would just get worse and worse. If I ran, things would probably get worse, but there was still a little chance things could get better."

"And a little chance is better than none," I say, nodding. "Believe it or not, I get that. Been there, even."

She raises her eyebrows. "No kidding?"

"Do I look like the kind of guy who's had it smooth?" I say, chuckling. "Yeah, I don't know how much Blossom told you about me, but I went through all that when I was younger. Before I met her, even."

I notice Sage glance past me to the house briefly, and I feel a pair of eyes watching me. That and the smell of fresh coffee tells me Blossom is in the doorway listening, but I pretend I don't notice.

"I was in the foster system," I say, watching Flora munch. "Parents were addicts. It got bad. I ended up spending as much time out of the house as I could. Before I ended up going down the rough path, when I was really little, I'd hit up the local library for free lunches in the summer just to get out of the house. The cafe barista noticed a bruise on me that didn't look like it came from playing, one thing led to another, and one day, social services was knocking on my door."

"Wow," Sage says.

"Didn't get much better," I say. "Bounced from house to house, and it got harder to place me when I got a record as a little rebel. There was this one guy who was the worst, though. Guy named Ronald. Not Ron, no, he *chose* to go by Ronald." Sage laughed at that, and I felt a little better by breaking up the grim tone of the story. "The guy drank like nothing I've ever seen. Anything could set him off. If I didn't make my bed the right way or if I didn't read his mind and know he wanted the floors swept, he'd just fly off the handle." I stare off into the waters for a few moments, then give my head a little shake, realizing I'm starting to dissociate. "I've pushed a lot of that out of my mind, and I don't think that's the best road to go down over breakfast, so I'll leave it at that. But yeah, I tried to run one time. Guy found me five miles down the road from the backwoods cabin where he lived. So, you did better than me, if that's any reassurance," I add with a smirk.

Sage can appreciate the grim humor-- there's something therapeutic about it.

"I would have tried again," Sage says, "if it weren't for her." She nods behind me, and I turn and pretend to be surprised at the sight of Blossom standing there with a mug of coffee steaming in her hand. She's smiling warmly down at me, and she makes my heart beat hard against my chest. She's dressed in an oversized t-shirt that comes down to her thighs, and her legs are bare, hair loosely tied back in a messy ponytail. She looks like she just woke up, and something about seeing her so comfortable makes me feel all the more attracted to her.

"Morning, gorgeous," I say in a low tone, and she smiles warmly at me. There's already a blush in her cheeks. I wonder how long she was back there before Sage glanced at her. She moves toward us and takes a seat by me and Flora, phone and headphones in her free hand.

"You've been busy," she says, giving me a playful smile and glancing between me and Flora.

"You have a budding chef on your hands," I say with a smirk. "Michelin stars in her future."

"Hi Mommy!" Flora says brightly, scooting closer to her mother as she finishes off her pancakes.

"Hi sweetie," she says as she hugs the girl to her. "Mommy can't wait to see the sugar rush this gives you. Good thing your sous-chef is unbelievably cute," she adds with a wink to me, and I mouth a half-serious "Sorry" back at her.

"Yeah!" the kid gushes enthusiastically, and I can't help but chuckle.

"There are a few in the microwave for you," I add to Blossom. "Still warm, if you want to grab some."

"I think I might just get to that," she says, crossing her legs. "I like to start the morning with coffee and a podcast. It's like a breakfast ritual."

"Coffee, something nice to listen to, and a peaceful lake to look at-- that sounds like a ritual I can get behind," I muse thoughtfully.

"Oh god, don't tell her you want to listen to podcasts, she'll talk your ear off listing all the good ones," Sage says, and Blossom rolls her eyes with a scoff.

"I'm not *that* bad!"

"I think that sounds like a nice way to top off the morning, actually," I say. "Let me get these plates cleaned up and I'll come join you."

I collect the empty plates from Flora and Sage, then head inside, feeling a smile that won't fade from my face. I haven't had anything like this in...as long as I can remember, if I ever had it at all. Is this what it feels like to bond with a family?

Is this what it means to be a father? A good one? Can I even be such a thing?

I'm getting ahead of myself. It's just breakfast, after all. Right?

I wash up the dishes in a matter of minutes, then go ahead and take Blossom's pancakes out of the microwave. I pour myself a mug of fresh coffee and make my way back out onto the porch, carefully balancing my armful.

Outside, I see that Sage has already commandeered Flora and guided her out to the banks of the lake, walking around and inspecting different shiny rocks on the shore with her. Sitting on the porch alone is Blossom.

She hasn't noticed me yet. Her legs are crossed, and she's leaning back on her hands as she watches her sister and daughter play together with a soft smile on her face. I see her earbuds in her ears, leading down to her phone. She's downright picturesque, and I feel my heart throbbing faster than ever. Blossom is something out of this world. She's more than I ever dreamed I could have, and every time I see her simply living her life, taking joy in the simple pleasures, it drives me wild for her.

I carefully approach her, and she glances up at me, smiling as I set the plate down beside her and take a seat. Leaning close, I pull one of the earbuds from her ear, and I put it in mine. I can hear a woman's voice speaking, and while I haven't listened to many podcasts, the tone of voice tells me exactly the kind of one it is. I start to pick up on the words being spoken...just as I see the smile start to fade from Blossom's face.

"The White Lilac killer has left his calling card in 17 different states, and there are no leads. Despite a $250,000 reward for information, there are no credible witnesses, and he's free to kill again."

"... If anyone has any pertinent information pertaining to the case of the White Lilac killer, please notify your local PD or email us at--"

I rip the earbud out and let it fall to my lap, pulling out the one Hunter is using, too. I hastily turn off the podcast as my heart starts to race wildly. I hadn't known that the episode up next in my queue was about the White Lilac killer. I was just happy to listen along and share my hobby with the man I love. But I can see by the darkening look on his face that it was absolutely the wrong audio to hear together at the wrong time. Even after seeing that lilac tree through the bathroom window last night, I was able to push all suspicion out of my head. And when I came out to see the impossibly wholesome scene of Hunter bonding with Sage and Flora so sweetly, it was so easy to pretend all my worries and paranoia were just that: paranoia. Unreal. Impossible. Too silly and coincidental to be real life.

At least not my life. I mean, I'm just a regular young woman. Sure, I've been through some seriously dark times, but stuff like this just doesn't happen to me. Only, there's no denying it now. If I can't put together all the pieces now, then I must be totally blind. Or willingly ignorant. Or in the deepest swamps of denial.

And I know from the look on his face that he's thinking about the same things. He's wracking his brain for an answer, for an explanation that won't send me running. He's trying to justify it in his head to make it easier to justify it all to me. But that's now possible. This killer on the loose…what he's done is unforgivable. It's abhorrent. Inhuman and inhumane. I swallow hard as I stare into the dark, cinnamon-brown eyes of the man I've spent five long years pining for. The man whose blood runs in my precious daughter's veins. That thought makes my head spin and my heart ache. Little Flora. The most beautiful and pure part of my world. She is too young and too good to find out the truth-- if in fact, this is the truth Hunter and I are dancing around right now.

I tear my eyes away from him to glance over at Sage and Flora. They're hunched over by the gently lapping waves of the shores, picking through the mud for smooth pebbles and little weeds. Sage is speaking softly to her, pointing things out and giving them names for Flora to repeat in her sweet little baby voice. There's pure joy and awe on Flora's face. Everything she sees, everything she touches-- all of it is unique and new and lovely to her. In her tight little universe, all new things are good things. She's always been brave, almost reckless or head-strong. I figure she gets that from her aunt. But maybe… maybe she gets it from her father.

And what else? What else could she have inher-ited from him?

I turn to look back at Hunter, and I know I can't wait any longer. For my sake, for Flora's sake, I have to ask him the questions burning in my heart.

But not here. Not in plain view of my sister and child. My eyes glance pointedly over to the cottage, and Hunter catches on. He nods slightly and offers me his hand to help me up. I don't take it. I stand up and walk briskly to the back porch, leaning against the wood-paneled wall with my arms crossed over my chest. I don't want to let the girls out of my sight completely, but I don't want to be too close, either. This is not a conversation they should be privy to, not even Sage with all her sardonic wit and wisdom beyond her years. No, this is my conversation to suffer through. Alone. No matter how badly it hurts. After all, I'm the one who fell in love with a possible stranger. I'm the one who fell into bed with a potential murderer, who happily made him the father of my little girl. Perhaps this moment, this dark intersection of soft, lilac-scented fantasy and hard, pungent reality, is my punishment. My atonement for being so naive.

As soon as Hunter joins me on the porch, he gives me an expectant, intense expression, as though he's waiting for me to take the first leap. So I take it.

"Who are you?" I hiss under my breath, never taking my eyes off of him.

The question seems to wound him like a knife to the chest, like I've knocked some of the air from his lungs. He scowls. "I'm exactly who you think I am, Blossom," he replies.

"Oh? Is that so? Well, that might not be a good thing for you, then," I answer icily.

"What I mean is that I am the same exact guy you met and fell for years ago. I'm the boy who stole from your neighbor. Who hopped your fence like a hooligan. The one you covered for. You saved my ass because...because you trusted me. Or so I thought," Hunter murmurs.

"Are you really that boy? You seem awfully different to me. And besides, you were never innocent. Not like I was. You were twenty-three, and you'd seen a lot more of the world than I had at that point. More even than I have now. I was just a stupid, naive, clueless little teenage idiot and you saw easy prey, didn't you?" I accuse softly.

Hunter blinks several times, looking totally taken aback by the accusation. He holds up both his hands in surrender, shaking his head. "Whoa. What? Where is this coming from? I never saw you as prey, Blossom. You know how I felt about you then. You know how I feel about you now, too. You were an angel to me, straight from heaven. But I never once thought you were gullible or stupid or whatever you're accusing right now," he insists. "I loved you because you were good and pure. Because you had a kind heart. Because you were beautiful. The same reasons I still care for you so much today. I never stopped loving you, Blossom. I swear."

I can feel a lump forming in my throat. "God, this is so hard to talk about. It's so hard to reminisce and pretend everything is sunshine and roses. Our love story isn't as sweet and serendipitous as I once believed," I tell him bitterly. "I had my suspicions, but I shoved them away. Even back then, I knew so little about you, about where you came from. I never asked because in my mind, it didn't matter. It was pointless. Irrelevant. All I cared about were the moments we spent together, holding hands and kissing and cuddling under the lilacs."

He takes a cautious step forward. "That *is* all that matters," Hunter asserts.

I shake my head. "No. No, it's not. You're hiding things from me, Hunter. Big, scary things you don't want to talk about, and that I haven't asked about because frankly, I was terrified to learn the truth. I should've known you were too good to be true."

"What are you talking about?" he asks, his voice low and rasping. There's a hint of a warning in his tone, but that only spurs me on with more vitriol. I have to get to the truth, even if it means digging too deep and scratching the surface of something truly horrifying.

"I'm talking about white lilacs, Hunter," I tell him meaningfully.

He pauses for a moment, then recovers. "What about them?"

I sigh and stomp my foot, getting frustrated. "Are you really going to make me say it?"

"Say what?" he demands in a harsh undertone.

"That you-- that you're-- *involved*," I whisper, glancing at the girls with worry. To my relief, they are still oblivious, playing in the shallow water and reeds.

Hunter stands up straight and crosses his thick arms over his powerful chest, looming over me with a dark look on his handsome face. "Involved in what, Blossom? If you want to accuse me of something, you have to be more specific," he says.

"Hunter, you wouldn't hurt someone, would you?" I choke out, a long-held breath gasping from my throat. My arms hang limply at my sides as I beseech him. "I know you had a rough time of it growing up, what with the foster homes and the abuse--"

"You think that because I come from a shitty background I must be a shitty person? Is that what you're implying here?" he asks, sounding defensive and almost hurt.

"I don't know! I don't know what to think or what to say or do right now," I hiss. "How am I supposed to feel?"

"About me?" he asks, raising an eyebrow.

I roll my eyes. "Yes. About you. About everything. About...what you do."

"What do I do, Blossom? Hmm? What is it you have in your imagination that you're blaming me for?" Hunter demands in a low voice, eyes flashing. I stick out my chin defiantly.

"Oh, so you're going to gaslight me now? Just pretend like all of this is in my head? You never answered my question, you know," I retort angrily.

"What question?" he growls.

"Would you hurt someone? *Have* you hurt someone in your life?" I repeat, glaring at him.

He takes a minute, staring up at the sky as though the clouds might open up and swallow him, letting him escape my interrogation. But that rescue never comes, and finally he looks at me and gives a shrug. "Maybe. Yes. If someone deserved it, I would," he answers quietly.

A shiver runs down my spine. "Okay. Like who? And what? And how?" I go on.

He sighs in exasperation, pinching the bridge of his nose. "Don't you remember the way we used to talk sometimes? About how there are just some people in the world who are evil? Come on, Blossom. I'm not the only one with anger. You wanted to see people hurt, too. The right people. The bad ones. Men who hurt women. People who abuse children. The people who hurt you and me," he says gruffly.

I can feel the color draining from my face. He's right. I did used to vent to him all the time about how restrictive and cruel my father could be. About how one time the town drunk leered at me and chased me home while I was riding my bike. I was only nine at the time, and he shouted all kinds of terrible sexual slurs and threats at me. I thought I'd buried that. But now Hunter was ripping up the sod and tearing the truth back out of the dank, decaying earth.

"We used to talk about making them pay," he adds, staring at me hard.

I gulp. "Kids say stupid shit sometimes. It was just talk," I answer meekly.

He groans and rakes his fingers back through his thick dark hair. "No, it wasn't just chit-chatting, Blossom. You meant it. I meant it. Both of us."

"I would never act on it," I reply in a trembling voice.

"That's you, then," he answers. "I'd never want you to act on it, anyway. You… you're too good for that kind of life. You're too good for that kind of world."

"So, what are you saying? That you do it so I don't have to?" I scoff.

He grabs my hands suddenly, holding them tight as he peers deeply into my eyes and nods firmly. "Yes, Blossom. That is exactly it. I do what I do so that I can keep the world a safer place for you. And for Sage. And for our daughter," he explains.

I tear my hands away from him and stumble back a step, nostrils flaring. "Don't you talk about my little girl that way. Don't you involve her in any of-- whatever it is you do," I snap.

Again, my heart aches to see the hurt look in his eyes. I hate this. Every part of this is like a knife wrenching into my very soul, but I can't just ignore it. Not now that I'm a mother.

"She's mine, too," Hunter says slowly and softly. "You might have kept her from me for five years, but you can't take back what you said about Flora being my daughter."

"I didn't keep her from you on purpose," I reply angrily. "I had no idea where you were. I looked for you, Hunter. But you were off doing god knows what while I was raising our child. And besides, now that I know what kind of man you really are, I have to-- I have to take her away. She can't be around you. It's too dangerous."

Pain and fury flashes in his dark eyes. "You can't. Please, Blossom. I've only just met her and I already adore her. You can't just rip her away from me before I even get a chance to know my own daughter."

"I am her mother. I am her guardian. Her *legal* guardian," I specify. "And I have to do what's best for her, even if...even if it hurts me."

"And you think she'll be safe with you? Really? You want to be a crime journalist, you say, but do you understand how dangerous that is?" Hunter protests.

I glare at him. "Right. It's much more dangerous to be the one reporting on the crime rather than the one committing the crime," I hiss coldly.

I see that muscle twitch in his jaw, the one that tells me he's pissed but he's holding himself back. I know he won't hurt me. Despite all the other horrors he might be capable of, I can sense beyond the shadow of a doubt that he'd sooner jump off a cliff than harm a hair on my head or our daughter's head. But the truth is, that's not enough.

"I-- you know I would keep her safe, no matter," Hunter insists. My heart sinks. I was hoping he would respond to my accusation with indignant denial, that he would set me straight and clear the air of any suspicion. But instead, he's just dancing around the subject. He's lying by omission. And suddenly, I know my worries are bound up in truth.

Hunter is essentially confessing to me that I'm correct, that I have the true suspect right in front of me. All my research, all my podcasts, all my preparation-- none of it could have prepared me for the truth. The reality that the man I love so much, the man who is the father of my child...is a killer.

Suddenly, it becomes absolutely adamant to me that we get out of here. I need to retreat. I need to leave this place, this horrid town of death and disappointment and decaying dreams. I have to get the hell out of Ithaca and go back home to Albany. The sooner the better.

Without another word to Hunter, I tear away from him and rush down the steps of the porch. As I approach the girls, Sage notices me first, and her smile fades quickly to a suspicious scowl. I widen my eyes at her but don't say anything. She catches on that something is very wrong, but we're in sync enough to know without mentioning it that we have to put on brave faces for Flora. So I somehow manage to reconfigure my face into some semblance of a smile and pick up Flora from behind, scooping her up into my arms. She lets out a delighted shriek and peal of laughter, surprised to see me. She wriggles around in my arms to hug me, her pudgy little legs wrapping around me as she rests her head on my shoulder. My stomach twists painfully when I notice the white lilac still tucked in her hair from earlier.

"Okay, little one, it's time to say bye-bye to the water," I tell her softly.

"But I have fun, Mommy," she protests, surprised.

"I know, baby, but we can always come back another time. Mommy needs to go home, okay? Are you ready for a long ride in the car? I'll buy you a big girl ice cream if you behave," I plead with her. I'm usually not the kind of mother to use bribery on my child, but this… this is an unusual situation, and it calls for unusual tactics.

I can tell Flora is upset by this news. Her little chin is quivering as she gazes out at the lake with longing. I give her a squeeze and a kiss on the cheek. "Come on, sweetheart. Can you put on a big, brave smile for Mommy?" I ask her softly.

After a big sigh, she nods. "Okay, Mommy. I be good. Bye-bye water!" she calls out, waving her chubby little hand at the lake.

Sage joins in, giving her a smile and adding, "Bye-bye, lake! See you later."

I mouth the words *thank you* to my sister as we turn and start marching back to the house. To my mingled horror and relief, Hunter is no longer standing on the back porch. He's nowhere to be seen at all. I can't imagine where he might've gone, because even when we get inside the house and start hurriedly packing up our stuff, I don't see him. I wonder if maybe he got pissed off and decided to go on a long walk or something.

At least, that's what I tell myself as I load up my little family into the car. Just as I'm buckling Flora into her booster seat, I notice the white lilac in her hair again. I reflexively reach to remove it but then stop myself, biting my lip. Flora looks at me blankly, like she has no idea why I'm staring at her so strangely. I quickly force a smile and decide to leave the lilac be. I just can't bring myself to take it away from her. Not yet, anyway. I close the side door and slide behind the wheel, taking a deep breath. With one last hard look at the cabin, I start the engine, nearly peeling out in my haste to get on the road. I drive for awhile in silence, my hands shaking and white-knuckled on the wheel as I try desperately to shake the image of that long, sharp hunting knife from my brain.

But just as I've put enough miles between us and the cottage to start to breathe a little, I notice that someone is most definitely following us a little bit behind. I know I'm paranoid and shaken up right now, but there's no denying it. There's a car tailing us, and for all I know, it could be Hunter, coming after me to take back what belongs to him. By force.

BLOSSOM

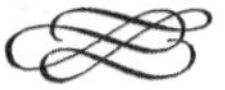

"Blossom, you alright?" asks Sage, jolting me from my panicked train of thought. I shake my head a little, as though to throw off my concern, and give her a weak, rather unconvincing smile in the rearview mirror. She quirks an eyebrow at me and tilts her head to one side-- a look I am extremely familiar with. It's as if to say, *Don't lie to me, sis.*

"I'm fine, yeah. Just, um, noticing some traffic starting to form way back behind us. I hope they don't catch up and start tailgating my car or anything," I lie, forcing a chuckle.

But my little sister knows me better than anyone. We have spent way more than enough time together for her to catch onto even my subtlest, most hidden changes in mood. I can tell she doesn't want to raise an alarm and risk scaring Flora, though, and I'm with her on that. My little girl is already kind of put out by our hasty retreat from the cabin, since she was having such a blast down by the water, and the last thing I need right now is to freak her out.

"Traffic, huh?" says my sister dubiously.

"Yep. Just some regular mid-afternoon traffic I'm concerned about. No big deal," I reply, giving her a meaningful look. Her brows furrow and her mouth sets into a hard line. She's catching on. I see her start to turn around to look out the back windshield very, very slowly. She yawns and lifts up her arms over her head as though she's simply stretching, so as not to alert Flora that there's anything going on. Far, far back, probably about a half mile behind us, is the same vehicle. Hunter's vehicle. Or at least, that's what it looks like from this far away. I can't be one-hundred-percent certain from this distance, but… I mean, who else would it be?

Sage bites her lip and gives me a subtle shrug.

"Does it look like...*traffic* to you?" I ask her pointedly.

"Hmm. Maybe. Should we be concerned about that for any reason? About the, uh, traffic, I mean? Like, is that a matter that should concern us right now?" she replies, careful to keep her tone light and breezy. I glance at Flora and I'm relieved to see that she is currently totally engrossed in counting the polka dots on her leggings. I can see her tiny rosebud lips moving, mouthing *three, four, five,* and so on.

"Well, I thought we'd left the traffic behind for a reason, you know?" I tell Sage, hoping that our makeshift code is intelligible between us. We have gotten pretty damn skilled at finding ways to codify our language so it's mostly undetectable by little ears, but this one is a bit of a stretch, especially because Sage probably has no idea as to why we actually left the cottage in the first place. For all she knows, Hunter and I could've just had a simple lovers' quarrel or whatever. That realization makes me shiver. I can't imagine how much she would panic if she found out the truth. How would anyone to react to that kind of revelation? I'm still not sure how I feel about it, myself, other than my need to put as much distance between my problems and me as humanly possible.

"Uh-huh. Gotcha. And, um, what reason is that, may I ask?" Sage presses me, folding her arms over her chest. Oh no. That's not a good sign. She normally only does that when she's getting annoyed with me. Clearly my sister isn't having as much fun with this little game of crack-the-code as I'd hoped. Still, I couldn't exactly lay out the bare, naked truth for her. Not here. Not now. Not in front of Flora.

Or ever, maybe. I mean, if Hunter really is who I suspect he is, who he confessed to be in a vague, roundabout way, then that's the kind of knowledge I should take with me to the grave. Right? I care about him deeply. That much I know for sure. And so of course my reflex is to want to protect him from harm. That means I have to keep his true identity and criminal rap sheet to myself, doesn't it? Then again, if he really is the wild, evil, out-of-control killer I suspect he may be, then would it be my civic duty to turn him in? Hunter implied in our hushed conversation that if (or when) he kills, he only kills those who "deserve" it. Bad guys. Evil men who make the world a dangerous place. So does that make Hunter a good guy? Does it balance out? Can he be both an avenging angel and a gentle, adoring lover? Can he be a hunting-knife-wielding vigilante and a tender-hearted father to a little girl all at once? I have so many more questions; some for Hunter, and some that no living being can possibly answer.

Sage loudly clears her throat in the seat behind me and I give her a hasty, sheepish smile in the rearview. She's waiting for me to give her a concrete reason as to why I'm worried that we're being followed. But I don't have a reason for her. Not one I can put into coherent words and give breath to. Ugh, why does this have to be so hard? I never hide things from my sister, but this time...it's different.

Isn't it?

That vehicle is still tailing us from a safe distance. Whether or not it's Hunter, I decide I want to shake them off somehow, so on a whim, I take the nearest exit to the right and start looking for residential streets. Maybe if I get off the blank, flat highway, it will be more difficult for my assailant to keep tabs on me.

"Why did you turn down this way?" asks Sage, leaning forward.

"Oh, I just wanted to get off the highway for a bit. It's so monotonous, you know. I get bored of it," I remark with false levity.

"So you knocked our journey way off course for...a change of scenery?" she asks flatly.

"Not *way* off course," I defend myself weakly. I turn down a few more streets to the right, following the rows of businesses and shops in search of a more populated area. Of course, the stretch of road between Ithaca and Albany isn't the most exciting or metropolitan route in the world, but even out in the country they have got to have supermarkets and stuff. Besides, we've barely made it past the outskirts of Ithaca's city limits. We're technically still in the metro area. But I want to be cautious about this and make sure I shake off our follower long before we make it much farther down the road. Who knows? It could be Hunter trying to follow us home so that he'll know where we live. The thought of him doing just that makes me want to cry. I hate thinking of him this way. I can't imagine him as a truly evil guy with evil intentions. That image just clashes so violently with the picture I have of him in my head.

Of the gentle, loving, doting man who cared for me so tenderly years ago.

Come on, Blossom. Focus.

I keep making random left and right turns until I find myself driving through cutesy, quiet suburban neighborhoods. There are kids out riding their bikes, dads in windbreaker jackets mowing the lawn, moms planting flowers. It's the epitome of a suburban, domestic paradise. It's almost enough to make me smile and forget about the harrowing escape we're currently engaged in. I can't help but wonder what it must be like to live in a place like this. Surrounded by a warm, predictable, dependable, stable cocoon. No worries, no fears. Just wholesome family comfort.

I shake myself out of it. That domestic daydream will never be my life. I will never have the kind of stability and completeness to make that happen. These suburbs are for families with two well-adjusted parents who make good money, for perfect, traditional, cookie-cutter family structures. I know what I have is pretty good. I love that my daughter gets to grow up between a mother and an aunt who love her and spend lots of quality time with her. I can keep a roof over our heads and food on our plates. That should be enough to settle for, right? Besides, clearly I can't be trusted to choose the right kind of man to round out my family. I always considered myself a damn good judge of character, especially once Flora was born and my maternal instincts kicked in. All this time, Hunter has been my ideal man, my prince charming. And yet, he's so much darker and more mysterious than I ever could have imagined. I guess the man of my dreams is more like the man of my nightmares.

So I got that wrong, too. I put us-- all of us-- in danger. Not anymore.

After about twenty minutes of weaving in and out of the residential streets, I look back again and realize with a sigh of relief that we're no longer being tailed by that vehicle. Up ahead on the left, I see a supermarket, a giant box store. I decide that's what we need right now. A little time to stretch our legs. Besides, I need to pick up something for Flora's lunch on Monday. Sage is a great caretaker, but she's never been much of a cook. So I pull the car into the lot and park as close to the entrance as I can, then turn the engine off.

"Where we going?" Flora asks, turning as far to the left and right as she can in her booster seat to look around.

"Good question," Sage murmurs, looking at me.

"The store! Just take it as a chance to stretch your legs, okay?" I reply brightly.

"Can I pick out a toy if I'm a good girl?" Flora gasps, her brown eyes wide.

I grin and nod. "Sure. Why not. Let's go."

"Yay!" she exclaims, kicking her pudgy little legs

as Sage unbuckles her from the seat. I come around to the passenger door and slide it open, lifting the little girl out. At first, I carry her on my hip as we walk into the market. I know she's more than old enough to walk around on her own, but I still worry. Especially with that close call. I don't want her apart from me.

Once we get inside, though, I relax a little. The market is bustling and packed, but everyone seems smiley and upbeat. Everyone is polite. I let my guard down, albeit reluctantly.

"Is it cool if I go look at makeup?" Sage asks me.

"Yeah, yeah. Sure. Just be careful. And keep your eye on your phone in case I need to get ahold of you. I'm just going to grab a few things. Won't be very long," I tell her as I grab a cart and slide Flora into the child seat.

Sage nods and heads off, walking briskly toward the beauty section. I can tell she's annoyed with me. She doesn't like when I keep things from her, even little things. Ever since we were children, we always shared every secret together. Sage is a tough cookie, and very independent. It's just in her nature to be a little prickly sometimes. But she's always been more vulnerable with me. I'm the only one she lets into her world. So I know it feels like a betrayal to her that I'm clearly holding something back. I make the mental resolution to come clean about it sometime. Maybe not soon, but someday.

I steer the cart toward the food aisles, humming some incoherent tune to myself as I idly shop. I don't have anything specific in mind. I grab a box of frosted flakes, some wheat bread, peanut butter, strawberry jam, carrot sticks, a gigantic bottle of apple juice, pretzels, and-- as a special treat for Sage and me-- a tub of roasted red pepper hummus. It's one of our favorites, and back when we first moved in together and we were really struggling to get by, we used to pool our meager funds at the end of the month to buy good hummus. Maybe it sounds a little pathetic to some people, but for us, it was just a delicious little pick-me-up to brighten up our grim days. Even now that we're closer to thriving than merely surviving, that hummus has a special place in our hearts.

As I shop, Flora plays with my hand, running her little fingers over it as I have my fingers wrapped around the steering bar of the shopping cart. She, like me, is humming and singing soft, nonsensical songs to herself. I make my way toward the ice cream aisle, wondering if there's any chance a pint of mint chocolate chip might survive the three-hour drive back to Albany without melting completely, I absently stroke Flora's soft brown hair. I'm just about to reach for a pint of ice cream when suddenly there's someone beside me, gently tapping me on the shoulder.

I gasp a little, clearly still on edge from what

happened this morning, and I whip around to face the squat middle-aged woman peering up at me with rosy cheeks and frosty white hair. She looks apologetic. "Oh! Sorry to frighten you, dear, but I'm a little lost," she begins, smiling.

"Oh. Uh, well, I don't work here or anything, but-_"

"I'm just wondering if you could point me to where I might find the cereal," she continues, still beaming up at me with that rosy grandma face.

I'm about to shake my head and move on when I remember that I actually do know the answer this time. "I did just grab some cereal, actually. It's just a few rows from the back. Aisle four, I believe?" I tell her.

"Ah! Thank you, dear. Much appreciated," she says sweetly, and toddles off on her merry way. I watch her go for a moment, then turn around to reach for Flora's hand again. But to my confusion, I seem to miss completely. I look over at the cart, bewildered, and my heart nearly sinks to the floor.

She's gone.

"No. No, no," I murmur, bile starting to rise in my throat. That's definitely my cart, and there's definitely no adorable five-year-old in it. "This can't be happening," I gasp, cupping my face with both hands. I start spinning around in frantic circles, then race up and down the aisles, calling out for her in a breathy voice. I can hardly get enough oxygen into my lungs to keep upright, I'm spiraling so fast.

"Flora! Flora!" I cry out, tears springing to my eyes. I only looked away from her for a second. How did this happen? Who the hell would do this? I don't know anyone in the area, and what would anyone want with a little girl, anyway?

Wait. I do know someone around here.

Hunter.

Could he-- *would* he have pulled something like this? Maybe he did follow me here. Maybe he did decide to take what he believes he's owed. Maybe he kidnapped his own daughter.

I didn't think she would be that good at trying to shake me, but this is the Blossom I fell for so long ago-- of course she has some unexpected skills up her sleeve, I should have known.

Scaring her was the last thing I wanted to do, of course, but I couldn't just let her walk out of my life with the wrong impression. I have to find her again and explain my actions. It isn't just because her running off like this leaves me with a huge risk to my identity to deal with. I don't want her to go. Legitimately, passionately, I don't want her to leave my life again. Not without getting a chance to let her see why I do what I do.

How could I not follow her? As soon as the three of them pulled off, I got in my car and tailed them from as far a distance as I could. There's only so much you can do to keep yourself from being noticed on these long woodland roads, so it was even more surprising that it wasn't until we hit heavier traffic that she seemed to notice me.

I won't hurt her, and it's painful to me that she doubtlessly thinks that's exactly what I'm planning to do. When you're alone with your fears, it's easy to start having imaginary conversations and getting riled up about them. During that tense drive, all I could think about was how she's probably comparing me to the dozens of other maniacs she's learned about over the years in those damn podcasts-- sociopaths with Freudian issues who kill just because they like feeling powerful and being able to get away with murder at the drop of a hat, getting off on the suffering of other people and asserting dominance.

That isn't me. I meant every word I said to Sage. I suffered through hell because the system wasn't enough to keep me safe when I was vulnerable. It hurt me, and it hurt Blossom. I started doing this because I stand up for what I believe in, and what I believe in is a safer future for everyone.

But getting Blossom to see that is another thing entirely.

She didn't actually shake me in traffic. I knew I was pushing her too hard, so I backed off and let myself disappear in the suburbs. It was a big risk, because it meant that for a while, she legitimately did have a chance of escaping my sights, but I found her again and tailed her at a safer distance the rest of the way to the store.

But I couldn't just charge in after her and make a scene. That isn't how I want any of this to go down, and considering that she's probably more than on edge already, doing something brash like that would make it a surefire thing that the police would get involved. From there, it would only be a matter of hours before I was handcuffed and getting shipped off to trial.

Whether she knows it, Blossom holds the fate of the Lilac Killer in her hands.

So, I circled around the store several times, eyes hounding the parking lot for signs of Blossom. I've spotted her parked car, so I know she's still here, but catching her as she comes out will be a different matter. Frankly, I don't even know what I'm going to do when I do see her. Veering in front of them in the parking lot would be just as bad as chasing them down in the store. I need to be careful about this. Not just for my sake, either-- Sage may or may not know what's really going on in Blossom's head, but Flora is definitely ignorant of the truth.

I don't need to be her father to know she should stay that way.

But just as I'm making yet another round of the block, I see that familiar face burst out of the entrance of the store. It's Blossom, her blonde hair looking frazzled and her eyes wild. She looks furious and terrified all at once, and I grip the steering wheel hard. What the hell happened to her? Without a second thought, I pull into the parking lot and stop the car a long ways from the entrance. She's clearly disturbed, and I don't want to scare her more by driving up close to her.

I check to make sure my knife is in its place in the sheath hidden beneath my pant leg, then climb out of the car. I start hurrying toward the parking lot aisle where Blossom is making her way through the cars, shouting, and then she sees me. I hold up a cautious hand to let her know I don't mean any harm, but she brushes away my worries the next second with the one thing I expected least.

She starts barreling down the parking lot toward me at full tilt, fire blazing in her eyes.

I'm so caught off-guard that I barely react as she closes the distance between us, and she throws herself on me, hands clutching my shirt. She tries to pull me toward her, but she ends up just pulling herself up to me.

"Where is she?!"

"Who?" I say, wide-eyed, putting a hand over one of hers and trying to calm her down.

"Don't fuck with me, Hunter! I swear to god, I'll get the fucking FBI out here in the blink of an eye if you don't tell me where she is," she shouts, and I can see real, primal anger in her eyes. I've never seen this side of Blossom before.

"I have no idea what you're talking about, Blossom," I say, trying to use the most soothing voice I can, but there are already tears in her eyes. Those eyes say a thousand words. They bore into me, sharper than the nails digging into my shirt, and they search me. It's like an hours-long interrogation taking place in complete silence in the span of just a second. But I know she can see the truth in my eyes.

I don't think we could really lie to each other, even if we wanted to.

Her face doesn't soften, but she loosens her grip on my shirt.

"Flora," she breathes hoarsely, eyes turning desperate. "Flora, she's gone, Hunter!"

"What?!" I say, and immediately, every instinct in my body kicks into high gear.

"She can't be far, I saw her last just a few minutes ago!" she says, letting go of my shirt.

"Did she get loose?"

"She was in my cart, she couldn't have gotten out without my noticing!"

"Someone took her," I snarl, and adrenaline starts coursing through my veins. Suddenly, I feel like I can see more intensely, every sense heightened as I take off running through the busy parking lot.

"FLORA!" I bellow, my deep voice carrying through the whole parking lot.

"Flora!" I hear Blossom's voice behind me. If only to help find her child, she can set aside her judgment and work with me. I would take that as a good sign, if I weren't busy feeling just as much urgency to find Flora as she is. After all, she's my daughter, too. And I'll be damned if I let some stranger harm a hair on her precious little head.

I dart through cars, bursting out onto the next aisle and hearing the sounds of honking horns and screeching tires as customers scramble to avoid hitting me. One comes close, but I hop over the hood and keep going without missing a beat. I worry for a moment that Blossom is going to chase after me, but she smartly fans out and covers the ground closer to the store.

The two of us fill the parking lot with our shouts, and after a few moments, I catch sight of Sage staggering out of the store, looking wide-eyed and confused. Blossom starts shouting the situation to her while I dart off further across the lot, shouting my daughter's name.

My daughter.

The idea of coming so close to reconnecting with Blossom and meeting Flora, my own flesh and blood, only to have her torn away from me…it fills me with a more pure and unrestrained fury than I've ever known in my life. What Blossom described sounds like a textbook kidnapping from public. A mother turns her head for half a second, and the child is gone. It's a nightmare come to life.

And if there's one thing I can say I've done with my life, it's take a little more of that nightmare out of the world and sent it to hell where it belongs. I'm going to find whoever took our child and tear him limb from limb.

Searching car to car, I see nothing. Every second that goes by feels like another inch toward oblivion. I stop and reach down to my pant leg to take my knife out, holding it at the ready as I whip my head around for a sign of anything. I keep running toward the far end of the lot, where employees normally park, and I stop dead in my tracks.

Lying in one of the empty parking spots is the little white lilac I tucked into Flora's hair at the cabin. I feel my fist tighten around the leather handle of the knife so tightly that my knuckles turn white, yet I feel like I'm seeing red.

She's gone.

We are too late.

I hear running footsteps coming up next to me, and Blossom comes to a halt at my side. She gasps at the sight of the flower, a more terrible, heart-wrenching sound than I've heard in my life. My eyes scan the area around the parking spot, but I see nothing. No sign of anyone, much less Flora and a kidnapper. I feel my heart sinking, and for the first time in a long time, I feel powerless.

"Mommy!"

The word hits us both like a lightning bolt, and our heads snap to a tree on a median not far from where we're standing. I stow my knife and race after the sound of Flora's voice so fast that I don't even realize my legs are moving.

I vault over a compact car and find Flora sitting on the curb of the parking lot, her knee scuffed and her eyes wide with fear and confusion.

"Baby!" Blossom cries, and she rushes past me to Flora, scooping her up in her arms and hugging her tight as tears flow from her eyes freely. I've never felt so relieved in my life, and I let a smile cross my face as I step forward and look into Flora's frightened face.

"It's okay, darling," I say, "we're here."

As soon as I say that, Blossom turns Flora's face from me, glaring at me with a face that tells me she hasn't forgotten the fact that we're not on good terms right now, but both of us know our relief over finding Flora overrides that for now.

"What happened to you, sweetie?" Blossom asks, holding Flora back enough to look her in the eyes. "Did someone hurt you?"

"A man was here," she says. The kid is clearly still jarred by everything that happened, unable to process all of it, but she's old enough to be very alert to her surroundings.

"A man! A man? Sweetie, what kind of man?" Blossom urges her in a trembling voice, more panicked by the second.

"He was big, and he picked me up," she says.

"What did he do, honey? Did he hurt you?"

She shakes her head, but she seems put off enough that she is at least partially aware that this was not a *good* man.

"He took me outside here," she says. "He clicked the car open with his key, but then he saw them and got scared." She points past us to a police cruiser that is stopped outside the store, idling. The cops are probably here on routine shoplifting prevention duty. They must not have even seen us running.

"The police cars?" Blossom clarifies. Flora nods her head.

"The kidnapper must have seen the cops and gotten scared," I say.

"He drop me, but I'm okay," she says bravely, looking down to her scraped knee. Blossom seems to have only just noticed it, and she gasps, quickly sitting down on the sidewalk, reaching into her purse and taking out a wet wipe to start cleaning it.

"Oh sweetie, I'm so sorry," she says, and I see her hand shaking as she tries to work. I calmly stoop down beside her and take the wipe from her. She looks up at me for a moment, hesitant, but I give her a nod and start cleaning up Flora's scrape. The little girl winces when the wipe touches her scuffed-up knee, but to her credit, she holds it together without so much as a single tear. She's one strong little lady.

"He's long gone by now," I say. "If he so much as suspects the cops saw him with Flora, he'll have run so fast I'm surprised he doesn't get busted with a speeding ticket."

"He drove real fast," Flora confirms.

"You're safe now, sweetheart," I say to Flora reassuringly, giving her a smile. "Now honey, I need you to listen closely, okay? That man was a bad man. Strangers who try to take you when your mommy isn't looking are bad people."

She nods slowly, her face clearly not entirely sure what to make of this new information, but she seems to accept it in stride.

"If that ever happens again, I want you to kick and scream as much as you can," I say slowly, gesturing with my hands to drive the point home. "Scream that it's not your mommy or your sister. Okay?"

"Okay," she says, and Blossom sniffs as she nods in agreement.

"I love you so much, honey," Blossom says, hugging Flora tight. The kid, blissfully ignorant to what almost happened today, simply hugs her back and giggles.

"I love you too, Mommy!"

Sage finds us, panting and out of breath, but she looks just as relieved as Blossom when she sees her niece.

"Oh thank fuck," Sage gushes.

"What does that word mean?" Flora asks Blossom innocently as Sage winces.

"She said 'duck', honey," Blossom says quickly, covering Flora's ears while narrowing her eyes at Sage, but she smiles the next moment. "Let's get back to the car. I'll explain in there."

We make our way back to Blossom's car, and even I can feel how awkward and tense the walk is. Blossom doesn't want to look back at me, but Sage keeps glancing between me and Blossom, knowing something's up. I get the feeling she hasn't told Sage what she has all but confirmed. I can't help but feel relief, but that leaves unanswered questions between me and Blossom. When we reach the car, Sage helps Flora get into the carseat and climbs into the passenger's side, closing the door while Blossom lingers by the closed driver's side door.

She's waiting for me to speak, or rather debating with herself whether she wants to wait. I make the decision for her.

"I was twenty-four," I say calmly. She looks up at me with a searching gaze, and I meet it, not a scrap of dishonesty in my eyes. "Almost a full year after you got taken away, and just a few months of being on my own in a new town. I hadn't gotten this job yet. I was working at a lumber camp for cash. It was the kind of place people went when they had to lay low." I run my hand over my face and take a deep breath, putting a hand on the trunk. "That was where I killed first."

"What happened?" she asks, her voice as defiant as it is curious.

"The foreman used to bring his son to work with him," I say, remembering the boy's face. "He couldn't have been older than fourteen. Frail boy. Wasn't suited to that kind of work. The foreman had problems at home with his wife. Everyone knew it, but nobody could talk back to him. The workers who took smoke breaks did it behind this old abandoned trailer at the camp. I headed back there to take a phone call one afternoon while I was cleaning up, and I caught them."

Blossom's gaze is fixed on me, deciding whether to believe what I'm saying. Given her career, I have no doubt she knows where I'm going with this.

"He was beating the boy with the flat of an old hand-saw. I don't know what set him off. I think he made a bad cut earlier that morning. Or maybe the foreman was just having a rough day. The boy was biting down on a rag, just taking it, tears in his eyes.

Getting hit all over his thighs and his stomach, places his mother wouldn't see."

I look over at Blossom without a shred of remorse in my eyes.

"We saw each other, but the foreman didn't even say anything. He knew I wouldn't talk. It would cost all of us our jobs. He just left with his boy." I take my hands off the trunk and let them hang at my sides, taking a deep breath. "I waited until his wife finally kicked him out of the house, tracked down the bachelor's motel where he was crashing, and caught him on his way to work one morning. That was before I started using the lilacs. The police haven't even connected that one to my profile. I'll be surprised if they even find what's left of him."

"Why are you telling me this, Hunter?" she asks, her voice so close to quivering with fear and yet so strong.

"Because I want you to know why I do what I do," I say firmly, taking a few steps toward her. She doesn't budge. "Because I want you to know I'm not some narcissist doing this to stroke my ego. I do it because people like my parents, like that foreman, like the man who tried to take Flora, they're out there and getting away with evil every day. Someone needs to be the bad guy who can bite back."

We stare into each other's eyes, both of us equal parts defiant and resolute.

"And if there's someone out there who wants to

hurt Flora," I say in a low, deadly tone, "I'm going to crush their skull with my bare hands...but we need to be on the same page. That, or you could call the police, and they'll be all over my ass before I'm halfway back to the cabin." I pause, looking into those beautiful, reflective eyes.

"So?" I ask. "What'll it be?"

BLOSSOM

*H*unter's story keeps pinging around in my brain, like a bunch of marbles rattling around a cardboard box. I can't seem to wrap my head around what he confessed to me. What he revealed. The side of him he's kept closed-off and private from the rest of the world. For a moment, I wonder if there's anyone else out there who knows the truth. If there's someone else he's confided in. But I can't imagine what type of person that would have to be. Hunter has always been fiercely independent and private. He wears a brave, nearly unreadable face, all the time. I know it's by design. You don't live through the kind of upbringing he had and escape totally unscatched and with your innocence intact. Hunter doesn't trust anyone, and I'm sure that kind of long-term paranoia and frustration with the way our world fails to reward the good and punish the evil is what pushes him into this dark, shadowy corner. It is easy enough to follow the exact trajectory that led him to becoming the White Lilac killer. The path he walks is littered with reasons, big reasons, solid reasons, for taking up the mantle of a vigilante for justice.

But those are just reasons, right? Not excuses.

It's a circular line of logic, I know, but I keep riding this infinite track back and forth between two ends of my reasoning. On the one hand, Hunter has straight-up admitted to me that he's responsible for at least one death, if not countless others. He has a death toll, and it's climbing ever higher. What's more is that he seems to bear no remorse for his actions. Hunter is not ashamed to have played the roles of judge, jury, and executioner for a bunch of random strangers. That should frighten me. It *does* frighten me. Of course, it does. I would have to be totally insane to look at Hunter with that damn hunting knife in his hand and not feel a twinge of fear. It's only natural. Humans may think they're complex, but underneath all the trappings of society and decorum, aren't we just frightened animals all desperately trying to stay alive and out of harm's way? Especially me. Because it's not just myself I have to worry about. There is a tiny, perfect, pure creature completely under my wing. Flora. I have to protect her from bad things, even if those bad things look so handsome and seem to care so much about her and me. That's my role as her mother: to protect her.

But on the other hand, if there's anyone in this world who is capable of protecting my little family, wouldn't it be a man like Hunter? He's agile and strong. He's clever and cautious, and yet he's reckless enough to throw himself in harm's way if it means protecting the ones he loves most in the world. And I know he doesn't have anyone else to love. No family. Probably no real friendships. I mean, I can't imagine that life as a traveling hunting specialist-slash-serial killer is particularly conducive to creating long-lasting friendships. All the love he has in his heart is reserved for me, and now for my sister and daughter, too. I can still see so vividly in my mind's eye the image of him doting on Flora, holding her, playing with her, making her laugh and smile so big. Hell, even Sage, who is notoriously stubborn and hard to crack, seemed to like him. He made her smile. He got her to talk a little bit. That has to mean something.

Don't be so foolish, Blossom, I think to myself sharply. I have researched more than enough true crime content to know that serial killers are often very good at charming and disarming people. It's why they're so dangerous, so insidious. They know how to smile and look normal, even when they're hiding a knife behind their back.

But I can't deny that what happened with Flora at

the supermarket has me pretty shaken up. I have had only a couple of moments during the past five years that were even remotely similar to the dire panic of a near-kidnapping.

One time, when Flora was just a little baby, maybe not even six months old, I was lying in bed listening to the baby monitor. I used to fall asleep that way every night, soothed to sleep by the soft, rhythmic sound of her snoring. And then suddenly, it was all too quiet. Silent, actually. Her breathing had stopped. I sat straight up in bed, petrified. I listened hard...and nothing. Terrified that my baby was in distress, I rushed into her nursery to see that she was sleeping soundly, her little chest rising and falling just as it should. As it turned out, the batteries in the monitor had simply run out, so the thing turned off. Another time, when she was just about to turn four, I momentarily lost track of her at a public park. I looked down for one second to send a text message to Sage, who was in a tizzy because she'd locked herself out of our apartment, and when I looked back up, Flora was nowhere in sight. I immediately freaked out and ran around screaming her name, no doubt traumatizing all the other kids and parents there that day. Finally, I found her sitting underneath a slide, just chilling out like nothing was wrong. Her explanation? It was hot out, and she wanted to go into the shade to cool down. I was so relieved to find her again, and even though she'd only been missing from my sight for less than a whole minute, it was enough to give me recurring nightmares for weeks afterward.

I glance up at the rearview mirror to see Flora's eyelids drooping a little. She's staring out the window, blinking slowly and yawning. I smile to myself, feeling my heart surge with affection for my little angel. "Sleepy, baby?" I ask softly.

It seems to take a lot out of her to turn and look at me, yawning. She nods. "Tired, Mommy," she says simply.

"It's been a big day," Sage agrees, stroking Flora's pudgy cheek.

"You can close your eyes and take a little nap, if you want. We'll probably be home by the time you wake back up," I urge her in a gentle tone.

"Okay, Mommy."

She shuts her eyes and leans her head against one side of the booster seat. Her pouty bottom lip pokes out as she almost immediately drifts off to sleep. Sage and I exchange looks of pure exhaustion. Even though she missed the bulk of our panic in the parking lot, I know this is wearing on her, too. It's a lot of work, both physically and mentally, caring for a little one. Most of the time, I feel like Sage and I are a dream team. But sometimes...I just wish we had someone else around to help out.

Like Hunter?

I swallow hard, trying to shake away that

thought. But the truth is, I don't feel safe with him, and I don't feel safe without him either. Still, when I notice he's still trailing behind us on the highway, I do feel a little thrill of relief. I guess that's my answer. For now, at least.

The rest of the three-hour drive goes smoothly. I stop once for gas, with Hunter doing the same, and thankfully Flora stays asleep the whole time, even when I have to start up the engine again. The poor little thing is totally worn out. I can't blame her. She was nearly kidnapped today. That's got to take a major toll on a tiny body. I find myself angrily wondering if she'll have to get counseling for this. Such a frightening experience could have a serious negative impact on her developing psyche. The thought that some strange man would put his filthy hands on my daughter with no regard for her well-being makes me want to pull over, get out of the car, and just scream at the top of my lungs. It isn't fair. It isn't right that evil guys like that even get to exist and breathe the same air as sweet, innocent children like Flora.

And now, in my burst of righteous fury, I can kind of understand where Hunter is coming from. His crusade to rid the world of evil bit by bit makes sense to me, even if I can't quite condone it. I understand it. I just can't abide it.

Or can I? Is life more complicated than I was taught? Are there infinite shades of gray between the stark black and white? Are the rules of society arbitrary or bendable in the face of such unfiltered, unabashed evil?

Either way, I'm too tired to come up with a sufficient answer right now. Soon, we cross over into Albany's city limits, and I sigh with relief. This city isn't perfect, but at least it's familiar. Plus, it's where my bed lives. And right now, I am desperate for a lie-down. As I weave the car in and out of the usual early evening traffic, I glance back to see that now Sage is resting, too. That puts a smile on my face. We're almost home, though, so she won't get much of a nap. Soon, we pull into the parking lot of our apartment complex, and while I'm backing into my usual parking space, I have to squint at a strangely familiar figure leaning against the outside of the building. It's not a masculine shape but a feminine one, small and slender. Skinny, with pointy elbows and a rather pinched expression.

Samantha, the homeless girl I talk to on my work breaks. I've given her my address multiple times to impress upon her that I have a couch she can crash on if need be, but she's never taken me up on it. As I wake Sage and take Flora out of her booster seat, Samantha starts slowly sauntering over, casting furtive glances in each direction. As though she's worried we might be watched. Sage yawns and gets out of the car, giving the homeless girl a nod.

"Hey Sam," I greet her warily. "What's going on? You look spooked."

She starts to ramble in a low, worried voice, "Sorry for showing up like this, but uh...I just wanted to warn you about something that happened earlier. At first, I wasn't going to, because it's probably just some guy being weird for no reason, and I didn't want to freak you out unnecessarily, but--"

"Dude. What's going on? Just spit it out," Sage says, walking over to put a hand on her shoulder. Although they've only met a couple times (Sage also comes by on my break sometimes to say hi), I think Sage sees kind of a kindred spirit in Sam. They're both young, fiercely independent, and have some admittedly rough edges to them-- Sam more so than Sage, but the similarities are apparent.

"So, earlier I came over here because I was already in the neighborhood and I wanted to drop in, maybe say hi or something. I realized you weren't home, so after I waited a while, I decided to leave," Sam explains nervously. "But as I was about to head out, this man stopped me to ask me questions."

I frown at her. "What kinds of questions?"

Samantha's eyes flit back and forth between us, and I can tell she's afraid to tell us. Just then, Hunter's vehicle pulls up just a few spaces away and he gets out, walking over with a dubious look on his face. Sam is startled when he shows up, but I put a hand on her shoulder.

"It's okay. He's with me," I assure her.

"What's going on?" Hunter asks.

Sage steps in to get him up to speed. "Sam here says that there was some guy hanging around earlier asking questions."

"Like what?" he growls, automatically on edge.

"Questions about...about Flora," Samantha says quietly, looking at me with wide eyes. My heart sinks and I can taste bile in my mouth again.

"What did he want to know?" Hunter demands, crossing his arms over his chest.

She takes a deep breath and answers, "He asked if Flora was home. I said no. So he asked when I thought she'd get home. I told him I had no idea. So then he told me that he's--he's Flora's father, and he wants to reconnect. But, like, he's super old, so I don't see how--"

"What?!" Sage, Hunter, and I all burst out at once.

"Her *father?*" Hunter hisses, anger flashing in his dark eyes.

"I know, I know. Obviously he was lying," Samantha says, rolling her eyes. "And don't worry, I didn't tell him a damn thing about Flora."

"What did he look like?" asks Sage.

Sam squints and chews on it for a moment, thinking. Then she says, "Old. Kind of big and burly. Like, stocky. He reminded me of a biker guy or, like, I don't know. A pirate."

"A pirate?" I repeat dubiously.

She sighs. "Yeah. Because he had this big tattoo on his arm."

"Was it an anchor?" asks Sage, half-joking. A flicker of a smile crosses Sam's face.

"No. It was a bird," she says.

Suddenly, Flora speaks up in her sweet voice and says, "That's the man who took me at the store, Mommy."

My stomach is twisting into nervous knots. Everyone focuses on Flora. "Sweetheart, are you sure? Did he tell you he was your--your father?" I ask her.

She shakes her head sleepily. "No. He didn't say nothing. He just grab me. I saw a birdie on his big arm when he carried me, Auntie Sage," she says. Sage looks up at me, horrified.

"Wait, someone took her? What?" Sam splutters, looking shocked.

"Long story," I murmur, too distracted by this new information. "Did he say anything else to you before he left, Samantha?"

It's like a lightbulb goes off in her head and her eyes widen. "Oh my god. Yes. He did. How could I forget the creepiest part?" she gasps.

"Well, shit," swears Sage. "What is it?"

Sam looks at me with an expression of pure apology and says softly, "He mentioned that he likes the new paint in Flora's bedroom."

For a moment, I'm so startled that I see black

spots crowding my vision, like I might just pass out from the shock and horror. "Holy god," Sage murmurs. "That must mean the guy has been inside the apartment. And recently, too. They've been painting the apartment over the weekend, so he must have gotten inside sometime from Friday and today."

"Is that how he knew how to find her?" I ask to no one in particular. Tears burn in my eyes as I turn to look at Hunter. He looks serious as a heart attack. He puts an arm around me and one around Sage protectively.

"Thanks for the heads up," Hunter tells Samantha.

"Don't mention it. I'm sorry to be the bearer of fucked-up news," she replies.

"Do you want to come in?" I ask her, worried. I hate the idea of her being on the streets, especially with some Flora-obsessed weirdo stalking around.

But just like every time I offer her help, she shrugs it off. "Nah. I'm good. Thank you, though. I'm gonna get going. Good night, guys. And...be careful," she says over her shoulder to us as she walks away.

Hunter starts guiding us toward the apartment building entrance, still glowering.

"Oh, we'll be careful, alright," he growls. "I won't let that man get anywhere near you. Not again. Not if I have anything to do with it."

HUNTER

Blossom looks like she's walking through a dream as we make our way to the bedroom that night. As soon as I close the door behind us, she sits down on the bed and buries her face in her hands, and her whole body shakes as she tries not to cry. It's been a tense hour or so since getting inside.

Sage was just as alert to what's going on as Blossom and I, so she didn't waste any time hurrying to whip up a quick but filling pasta dinner for all of us to keep the girls distracted. We spent the time letting Flora show us around the apartment while Sage cooked, and Sage offered to take care of Flora's bedtime routine while Blossom got some rest.

I had to admit, she was in the running for the Sister of the Year award.

"Hey," I say, sitting down next to Blossom and

gently snapping her out of her trance. She looks up at me as if she isn't even sure I'm here. I take her hand and squeeze it softly. "We're going to be alright. We're going to keep Flora safe."

"No child should have to go through this," she says, sniffling. I nod, closing my eyes and frowning.

"We won't let her," I say. She looks up at me, and I know that word *we* is what she's not so sure about. My frown deepens. We still have a lot to work through, and I can't blame her. "Blossom, I know you're not sure about having me here. I had a long time to come to terms with what I choose to do. You've only had a day. If you want me to go, I'll understand, but-"

"I didn't say I want you to go," she says in a quiet but firm voice. I pause, surprised. "Yesterday, every-thing in my life made sense. Now, I'm between a rock and a hard place. I don't even know if I know the real you. I've spent so many years studying people who live these secret lives, and I never thought one could be so close to me. That's what they all say, though," she adds bitterly, shaking her head.

"Do you think I'm like them?" I ask her simply, no anger in my voice.

She's silent for a few long moments.

"I want to say no," she says at last. "I want to trust my gut and think I know the real you, Hunter. I want that so fucking bad. Do you have any idea how hard that is, after everything I've been through?"

"I can never live your life, no," I say, and I take her hands in mine. "But I know that I need to make myself better for you. I never knew I was going to see you again, much less that I'm...a father," I finish, still not used to that word on my lips. "I want to make myself better for you. For Flora. Whatever that means. And I need you for that."

"And I need you," she says. "I don't know who this bastard is who's coming after Flora or why...but that's not the only reason I want you here." She bites her lip, and she couldn't look more beautiful in the dim lamp light of her room. "You were right, what you said at the cabin. We need to finish what we started. I'm afraid of all this, of everything we have, but I don't want you to go away. I've never felt this way in my life, and I have no fucking idea what to do with it all."

"Good," I growl, leaning in, "then we're on the same page."

I lean in and press a kiss to her lips. I feel just a second of debate in the tension of her body before she melts into it, and our hands slide around each other almost at the same time. I feel her hands run along my strong, hardened abdominal muscles, feeling up every inch of my body and tracing around the lines of definition I've worked so hard to perfect over the years. I've turned my body into the perfect killing machine, and knowing that she gets to enjoy that brings me more joy than any workout could. Our lips press against each other fiercely, and I invade her mouth with my tongue. It slips past her teeth and brushes against her warm, wet tongue, and I push my body forward to gently move her back down onto the bed.

I start stripping clothes off. First her, then me. We don't let ourselves break away from each other, grinding and groping, and I soon feel my manhood as hard as a rock between my legs. I squeeze her bare ass as soon as I expose it, then work the rest of her clothes off before she starts pulling at mine, urging me to do the same. Within a minute, all our clothes are in a useless pile on the floor. The moment I'm naked with her in the privacy of her room, our motions spill into primal, aggressive desire.

My hands slide up and down her sides as I straddle her, a knee on each side, and I bend over her to kiss her neck. My lips brush up and down the sensitive skin, and she squirms, feeling it tickle her. Seeing a smile on her face makes me happy, and I keep going, letting my teeth nip her and threaten the soft skin between sharp edges. Meanwhile, my hands move up to her breasts, and I squeeze her.

Her nipples are getting stiff, and my thumbs are only teasing them harder. The give her breasts offer me is irresistible. I cup them in my hands and feel their shape as we push our hips together, teasing one another as our legs slide lazily against the clean, fresh sheets. I hear her whimper as I start circling my thumbs around her areolas, and she pushes her chest up for more.

We know who we are in these moments together. We're two lovers who were torn apart, and now that we're back together again, we couldn't leave each other if we wanted to. Our lives have grown so far apart, and yet they've come so close. It's a hot mess of desire, and knowing Blossom like I do, I wouldn't have it any other way.

I move to the side and slide my arm under her from behind, pressing my cock against her taut ass so that it sticks up, its soft underside grinding against her cheeks while both my arms wrap around her front. My left hand goes to one of her breasts, where I start gently pinching and teasing the now-stiff nipple. My right hand slides down to her pussy.

She's already wet, and that makes me smile. The adrenaline earlier is a high unlike any other, even if the circumstances are horrific. That energy has to go somewhere, and that's part of what's fueling us right now. We know that we might not live to see tomorrow, and that's partly terrifying, but it's also thrilling beyond anything I hoped to feel in these long, lonely five years away from the love of my life.

Can I even call her that?

I don't know, but right now, that's what's burning in my mind. Love.

I push my hips back and forth, grinding my shaft between her asscheeks while my thick fingers find her little swollen clit, and as soon as it touches it, she gasps, clenching her ass and shuddering as if touched by fire. Her nipple stiffens even harder, and I smile, brushing the short hairs of my beard against her neck before I start peppering her with kisses. I move my hand in little circles around her clit, not wanting to deny my Blossom anything.

I've never felt closer to a person than right now.

There's something about lying in bed on our sides, letting my hands roam her and grope her freely, nothing occupying our thoughts right now than pure desire. It puts me at ease, fools me into thinking for just a moment that we have this life together, that there's nothing to worry about. No threats, no problems, no death, just us. That fantasy is a hot fire under us.

Her whimpering voice is music to my ears as I touch her, getting faster and more steady as I find the perfect rhythm for her. Her body tells me when to go faster and when to be firmer or gentler. I listen to it as if I was made to. If my body can't please her exactly like she needs, what's the point of honing it in the first place?

She starts to breathe more heavily, chest rising and falling while I toy with her breast, so I hug her tighter to me. My cock throbs against her, eager to enter something, but I'm not going to indulge it until

I feel her come. My rhythm is relentless and steady, so much so that it makes her squirm and whimper as I drive her further and further.

Finally, her mouth falls open, and I feel her whole body pulse as her first orgasm hits her, a wave of release spreading out from her clit to the rest of her body. I can feel it in the smooth cheeks pressed against my cock, and it's such a satisfying experience that even I can share in it.

She has hardly stopped shuddering in delight when I pull myself away from her. I lean against the headboard, sitting up, and she turns to look at me with lidded yet curious eyes. I grab her by the hips and help her up onto me, spreading out my thighs so that she has a firm seat to get steady on, facing away from me. She realizes what I'm doing and quickly helps get into position.

The sight of Blossom's ass in front of me, my stiff, girthy cock poised right at the swollen lips of her pussy, is alone almost enough to break me. She's the most beautiful woman in the world, and I've got her here in my lap to do whatever I want with her.

That makes it all the more satisfying when I slowly slide her onto my cock. The gasp of pure delight she gives as her warm lips move down the bulging crown to the vein-ribbed shaft to the very base of my cock is exquisite. Finally, she comes to a rest on me, letting her head fall back, golden hair teasing me. I chuckle and reach up to take hold of it, gently pulling her hair back, and she seems to like that. A lot.

We don't even talk. I don't know if we could focus our minds that much if we wanted to. The only thing I can think about right now is raw, primal rutting, and the way she's acting, I think she has the same idea.

She puts her hands down in front of her and starts to work her hips up and down in time with my gentle thrusts upward. I don't want to hurt her, but I remind myself that this is Blossom. She has a taste for getting rough, and I like that. I start getting more aggressive with how I thrust up into her, reaching around her soft hips and squeezing her in place. She helps me move back and forth, but even from below, I'm in complete control. If I want her to go faster, I start using my powerful, defined forearms to make that happen.

Each time she slides up and down, I see my cock, bulging with desire under her perfect ass and thighs. Soon, I can't stand not being able to touch her breasts, as much as I love her hips. I slide my hands up, releasing her hair so I can hold both breasts. I push myself up higher so that she sits more easily on my cock, and she slides her hands back to feel the thick, defined V of my hips and move herself up and down while I grope her.

"Fuck," is all she can breathe out desperately as I pound into her, squeezing her breasts and tormenting her nipples. I feel her starting to get tighter around me, clenching her pussy as tension starts to swell up like a string in need of getting plucked. I get fiercer, thrusting up into her relentlessly, pistoning up and down and moving my hands back down to her hips. I squeeze her, making her feel like she has no escape from me, no rest from my endless lust. I'm going to make her feel satisfied in the hands of a killer.

Soon, she can't even control her own body, and I feel like she's entirely mine to fuck as hard as I like-- and that's exactly what I do. I feel her start to quiver in my grasp as she gets closer and closer. Her mouth is frozen open, and she arches her back as my cock grinds against her g-spot and breaks the tension holding her back.

She comes so hard that her body feels like it melts against me. I clap a hand around her mouth to keep the sound of her groan from traveling too far, and the restraint seems to make her orgasm even more intense. I feel her pulsing all around me, slick honey surrounding my cock as I glide in and out of her with expert precision. I don't let up or lose control for a second. The body tries to squirm away from sensations like this, but I make her confront those ecstatic feelings as her body convulses on my cock.

When it finally slows down, I let my hand off her mouth and slowly push her off my cock. She puts her hands ahead of her and crawls forward, flopping down and panting on the bed, blushing beautifully. She cracks her eyelids open and looks at me with warm, loving blue eyes that melt my heart.

I crawl up forward after her, our heads at the foot of the bed, and I scoop her up into my arms. She giggles as I cuddle her close to me, and even though my cock is still stiff and needy, I take a moment to just *be* with her while she cools down. Her blushing face is the most beautiful thing in the world to me. We smile at each other, finally able to push everything else away from the two of us. But even as she stares into my eyes, her hand reaches down and wraps around my cock. She plays with it idly as she watches my massive chest rise and fall. I hear her give a satisfied murmur, and I move forward and kiss her.

Her lips are warm and delicious, and our tongues flirt with each other briefly before I pull away and get one more look at that picturesque face before I start kissing it on the nose, the cheeks, the neck, everything I can find, until she's a giggling mess. My hands go to her sides, and I rub her up and down, feeling her softness as she wiggles in my grasp.

Finally, she's ready for more. I gently turn her over onto her back, and I rub her quivering legs before sliding my hands under them and raising them up to my shoulders. I bend her backward until her legs are sticking straight up, and I watch her lick her lips as she watches my cock push against her slick lips.

"Are you read?" I ask in a thick, husky tone.

"I've been ready for so many years," she breathes.

I impale her with my cock, burying it deep into her, and she grips the sheets with both hands as I start to rut into her. I'm not holding anything back this time, letting my muscles work almost on autopilot, rocking back and forth with greater speed each time. I feel my balls so heavy and ready for release that my precum is already beading up and spilling out of the thick tip of my cock. I'm overflowing with love for her, and I need to pour it out into her soon before it all comes spilling out on its own. It feels like a fire inside me forcing its way out. That risk spurs me on and excites us both, because I know she can feel me in there.

I hold onto her hips and start using her to buck into fiercely, and something about that untamed ferocity starts to get her tense again in the same way my measured, relentless precision did minutes ago. Any way I use my body, it excites her, as if we were made for one another. Or rather, we've grown to be good for each other over the years, even in those years that we're apart.

I can't pretend to explain what it is between the two of us that works in tandem and feels so right, but it's a force that neither of us could resist if we wanted to.

My release is coming soon, and I make sure that she's right there with me. I have such a command over her body that I know just how to thrust into her to drive her closer and closer with every thrust. She starts to pant, gripping the sheets and clenching her eyes shut as I pound into her. My balls start to tighten, and I know I'm about to fall over the edge. She opens her eyes to see my concentrated, pained face, my rippling muscles gleaming with sweat in the lamplight, and that tips the scales for her.

She arches her back, and we come together. I feel such a forceful orgasm that my legs shake, despite all the powerful muscles holding my body up. The seed shooting out of my long shaft feels white-hot, and the feeling of release puts my mind in a spinning, heightened place that's even better than the high adrenaline gives me. Shot after shot, my body contracts to give her everything I have in blissful release, plastering the insides of her with my seed. She gasps and writhes with her orgasm, tears running from her eyes as she gets so overwhelmed she almost laughs. The smile on her face touches my heart, and in that moment, I know what it means to be madly, wildly in love.

We rest, panting in the dim light as we stare at each other. I bend down and kiss her on the lips, a long kiss we draw out as much as we can before we break apart and roll to the bed, exhausted.

"Let's get you cleaned up," I say at last, my voice still thick and husky.

"Yeah," she breathes. "Yeah, that sounds…really good."

~

The next morning, I lean back in the chair at the kitchen table, full of the breakfast I cooked. Blossom and Sage are doing the same, while Flora only managed to eat two thirds of the massive plate I set in front of her, and she looks at the rest of it with wide eyes, as if she has never had to face such a challenge before.

"So…we're going to hire him as a live-in chef, right?" Sage asks Blossom at last before forcing herself to stand up and collect our plates. Blossom laughs as she carries them to the sink to start cleaning up.

"I can get that," I offer.

"Not if Blossom and Flora want to start the day on time," Sage replies, and I raise my eyebrow at Blossom.

"What time does your shift start?"

Blossom jumps in her seat, looking at the time and holding back a curse. "Too soon. Let's get going! Flora, honey, let me grab your lunch real quick."

"I'm so full my tummy gonna 'splode," Flora says in awe, apparently at peace with death.

Five minutes later, miraculously, the three of us are in the car as I pull out and start driving Blossom to work.

"You look cute in that uniform, you know," I say with a smile. She rolls her eyes, plucking at the uncomfortable apron ruefully.

"I can't wait to throw this thing in a fire."

"We'll make s'mores," I say, chuckling.

"Yeah!" Flora chimes in from the back, excited, and I grin over at Blossom.

"See? We're committed now."

It only takes a few minutes to get Blossom to work, and I pull up to the side of the road and let her climb out of the car.

"Are you sure you're okay driving her to school?" she asks, just shy of wringing her hands. "Despite what Sage says, I really don't want to turn you into the errands guy."

"I don't feel like the errands guy," I say, flashing a smile back at her. "But if you get me a coffee when you get off work, we'll call it even."

She smiles and blushes at me, then lets herself laugh before shutting the door. I see her mouth "Drive safe!" at me as she waves, and Flora waves goodbye to her as I pull away.

I drive in silence for a few moments. The school is a little farther, but to say I don't mind getting to do something as simple as driving my daughter to school is an understatement. After a few minutes, I glance into the rearview mirror and see Flora staring out the window.

"Still feeling that breakfast, kiddo?" I ask, smiling.

"I want bacon forever," she replies, and I can't help but laugh. But after a few more moments of silence, she speaks again.

"Do you like Mommy?"

I feel my heart catch in my throat, and I don't know what to say at first.

"Yeah," I say at last. "You could say I like your mommy. She's pretty great."

"She's the best," Flora agrees, as if stating a simple fact. "She like you a lot. You're like best friends."

"We used to be best friends a long time ago," I say.

"I'm glad you friends again," she says. She can't possibly know what she's saying, but I find myself trying to push my heart down my throat again.

"Yeah," I say at last, feeling choked up. "Me too." Another pause. "What about you, huh? Any thoughts?"

"You're the biggest man I ever seen," she says as if commenting on a monument, and I snort a laugh. "Also, you make breakfast better than the place Mommy takes us on Sunday. So I like you."

I can't keep the smile off my face.

"Thanks, kiddo. You're pretty cool, too."

"I know," she says mildly. I hope she keeps that nonchalant self-confidence forever.

We fall into silence again, but I keep glancing at the rearview mirror. My smile starts to fade into a frown as I turn yet another corner through the quiet suburb, and as I watch the car a ways behind me follow me yet again down this twisting path I've been detouring through, it confirms my suspicions.

We're being tailed.

"Hey, kiddo?" I ask, still keeping an eye on the car tailing us.

"Yeah?"

"What do you think about skipping school today?"

Her eyes go wide.

"You can do that?"

"Only with your parent's permission," I say calmly. "So let's go see what your Mommy thinks, how about that?"

know I should be more cautious. I know I should slow down. But all morning, it's like I've been floating around on cloud nine, my toes barely brushing the ground beneath me. I have had the same dopey, lovesick smile on my face ever since breakfast this morning. There is just something so beautiful, so wholesome, about seeing the man I adore interacting so sweetly and naturally with my sister and daughter. I used to worry that when (or if) I ever eventually brought a man home to meet my unconventional little family, it would be awkward. I mean, Sage and I have kind of a system worked out by now. We work together seamlessly, sharing responsibilities around the apartment, the bills, the cleaning, the cooking-- all of that. And most importantly, the two of us know exactly how to balance it all with taking care of Flora. She is the centerpoint of everything, the hinge upon which every other factor turns.

I always imagined that introducing some random guy into the mix would just create a series of train wrecks. That perhaps having a man around would distract me from my duties as a mom, or that Sage-- who is notoriously choosy about who she deems worthy of her approval-- would resent having him around. Maybe Flora wouldn't like him, or she would be afraid of him. Or worse, that I would accidentally introduce someone dangerous into my little world and put not only myself but my sister and daughter in jeopardy. Dating, under even the best of circumstances, can be fraught with challenges and pitfalls. Dating as a single mom throws several wrenches into the mix. And then, of course, there's the obvious elephant in the room: that Hunter is no ordinary potential boyfriend. He and I have a long history together. He knew me back before I ever moved to Albany, before I became a mother. Back when I was just a modest, shy, sheltered small-town girl picking wild berries and dreaming of running away.

As I chat mindlessly with customers, sharing tepid small talk and ringing up their orders, my mind is far away. Physically, I'm stuck in the present moment here in the Lazy Bean, but mentally? I'm way off in the future, daydreaming about how beautiful things could be if they would only work out the way I want them to. For once, I can look to the future and see a faint, glorious glimmer of something beautiful waiting for me out there. My fantasies are mostly domestic these days. I would love to move out of our cramped apartment, maybe get out of the hustle and bustle of the city. We could find a place with a yard. Sage has always had a green thumb, but it's hard to keep much of a garden when you live in an apartment several floors up from the ground. She could plant herbs and vegetables and flowers, teach Flora how to care for delicate plants and get her hands dirty. I could quit this dead-end job and go back to school to study my passion: crime and journalism. I could finally work toward the kind of career I've always dreamed of.

Hunter would keep us safe, wouldn't he? I would never again have to lie awake imagining all the millions of things that could go wrong. Being a parent, especially a single mother, means constant worry. He could drive Flora to and from school. If she ever had a mean teacher or a playground bully, between the two of us, Hunter and I would set them straight. Nobody could touch us. Flora would have a mother and a father who love her and want what's best for her. Sage could finally take a step back and start living her own life a little more. I know she's content to stick around and help out, but for how long? She's nineteen, and she's had the same restless spirit since she was a little girl. Surely there will come a point when she needs to spread her wings and fly. And if I have Hunter around to pick up the slack, Sage can do just that.

We could be a real, functional, loving family. My little girl would grow up knowing how safe and protected and deeply loved she is. We would support each other through the good times and the bad, smiling through it all, knowing sunshine is just around the corner.

That's all I want. And I can't deny my feelings for Hunter, either. When I look at him, my heart flutters like a bird bursting free of its cage to take to the skies. When he touches me, every nerve in my body is on fire. I'm just as hot for him now as I was back when we used to roll around together under the lilac blossoms. I'm so blissfully happy imagining what could be that I can almost push away that nagging concern as to Hunter's vigilantism. Sure, the man I love treads along the sharp edge of a knife. He lives dangerously. And there are those who would condemn him for what he's done. But right now, all I can think about is how soft he is with Flora. How gentle. And how fiercely he will protect our family if I only give him the opportunity to prove it to us. He could guard us with his strength, keep us from harm...

I'm so deep in thought that it's not until he's all the way up to my cash register, scowling with disdain, that I recognize the customer in front of me.

It's the same asshole from Friday, the one who bitched me out for being distracted at work and got Marty all up in my business. And he doesn't look like he's feeling any more charitable and patient today than he did then. In fact, as soon as he steps up to me, he rattles out a long, heavy sigh. I haven't even said hello yet and he's clearly already sniffing for trouble. Some guys just can't control themselves, I guess.

But I'm at work, and even though my manager Marty's not here today, he's got one of his favorite sycophants, a middle-aged woman named Helen, keeping tabs on all the employees on this shift. Myself, included. I have to keep it together.

I greet him with a cheery, "Good morning! Welcome to the Lazy Bean. How may I--"

"Drop the spiel, alright? I already heard it once. What, you don't recognize me from five minutes ago?" the man grunts, glaring at me. I feel my face go ashen pale as it hits me that I must have been so zoned out on autopilot that I didn't even notice his familiar face when he came through my line the first time. I hoist up my fake customer service smile and try to do some damage control.

"Oh! I'm so sorry. You placed an order earlier, didn't you?" I ask.

"Yeah, that's what I'm saying. You were too distracted to pay attention, just like last time, and you got my order all wrong," the man growls. "You got some kind of brain problem?"

"Uh. Not that I know of. My apologies, sir. Could you tell me your correct order again so I can have the barista make it for you the right way? It'll be on the house, of course," I add quickly, looking at him with almost pleading eyes. I notice now something I must have missed before. It's definitely the same guy, but he looks… off, somehow. His skin is all blotchy and yellowish under one eye, almost like he's wearing a thin layer of makeup to hide a bruised eye.

"I want a large black coffee. Half decaf. With just a dash of soymilk. That dairy shit fucks up my stomach. You could've poisoned me with this cow's milk crap," he accuses, holding up his old to-go cup. I gulp hard. He's right. Maybe he's lactose intolerant or has a dairy allergy or something. I'd be pretty grumpy about that, too. I decide to try and cut him some slack. Between the wrong order and the messed-up eye, he sure looks like he's had a rough time.

"Yes, sir. I've got that coming up," I tell him cheerfully. "So, how are you today?"

"Hmm?" he grunts, frowning as though he's never been asked that question in his life.

I falter a moment. I had totally expected him to just answer the question. I mean, has this dude never encountered small talk before? What a weirdo.

I continue on, injecting as much sympathy into my tone as possible and gesturing subtly to his eye,

"What happened there? Are you okay? It looks a little painful."

His jaw twitches and his beady eyes narrow at my apparently too intrusive line of questioning. He sniffs disdainfully and averts his gaze, replying gruffly, "Yeah. Just had a bad fall, that's it. None of your business, by the way."

Wow. What an ass. It takes a monumental helping of self-restraint for me to tug my mouth into a polite smile again and reply, "Sure. Of course. Well, your order should be ready down at the end of the bar. Have a great day, sir!"

"Hmph," he grunts in response before shuffling off. I frown after him, a shiver running down my spine. Something about him just puts me off. There's something really weird about that guy. But now I have another customer coming up to me, so I tear my eyes away from Mr. Black Eye and get back to work.

Moments later, I happen to look over during a brief lull in the busy hours and catch sight of the nasty guy leaving...just as another familiar face comes walking in. It's Samantha, and even though the guy doesn't seem to notice her (as many people seem to flat-out ignore homeless folks like her), she sure as hell notices him. She even stops and stares for a moment in the doorway, turning slowly to watch him shuffle away down the sidewalk before turning back to make intense eye contact with me.

Seeing that there's no one else in line at the moment, Sam comes rushing over, looking pale and freaked out.

"Hey Sam, what's up? You look like you just saw a ghost or something," I greet her quietly. I glance around to make sure that busybody Helen isn't hovering over me. To my relief, she must be off in the bathroom or something.

Samantha leans in close, her whisper taking on a conspiratorial tone as she bursts out, "That's the guy! Are you okay? The asshole who--"

"Who? That dude who just left? Oh no. I've been serving him for years. Don't worry about him. He's annoying and rude, but he's harmless," I assure her.

But her wild-eyed panic doesn't subside with my explanation. "I'm telling you, B. That's the guy you should watch out for," she insists. I'm starting to wonder if she has her facts straight. Or perhaps-- and this is not a prospect I feel great entertaining-- she's just making it up. I don't think she would lie to me, but who knows? She's just a kid, anyway.

But just as I'm about to ask her to calm down and take a seat somewhere, the front entrance chimes again. This time, I do a double take at the figure walking into the Lazy Bean. My heart skips a beat at the sight of Hunter walking in-- carrying Flora in his arms, no less! Sam catches the stunned look on my face and spins around to see them there.

"Oh shit," she murmurs, catching on that something must be terribly wrong.

Hunter comes marching up to the counter, looking solemn, even though Flora looks positively tickled to be hanging out with him instead of in a kindergarten classroom. "Hey, are you alright?" he asks me in a low, furtive tone.

"I was just asking her the same thing," Samantha remarks, leaning on the counter.

I look back and forth between them, shrugging. "Yeah. I'm good. What the hell is going on here? Why isn't Flora in school?" I ask, keeping my voice quiet.

"Mommy say a bad word," Flora whispers accusingly.

A flicker of a smile crosses my face. "Yes. That's right. Mommy did say a bad word."

"*Hell*," she whispers, barely audibly. A mischievous grin brightens her face.

"No, no. That's a grown-up word. You can say that when you get a little older, okay?" Hunter tells her gently before turning back to me. "We had a little incident on the way to school, and I wanted to drop by and make sure you're alright."

"Why wouldn't I be? What's going on?" I ask, utterly bewildered.

"Someone was tailing us, Blossom. There was a car following me to drop off Flora at the school earlier. I decided it might be prudent for her to skip class today, under the circumstances," he tells me grimly.

"That's what I'm trying to tell you," Samantha insists, sighing. "That guy that was here earlier-- he's the one who was sniffing around your apartment looking for Flora. I'm tellin' you, that's your man."

"No. That--that just doesn't make sense," I breathe, starting to feel ill.

"Blossom, I think we have to start coming to terms with the fact of the matter here," says Hunter. "Someone out there really is trying to kidnap our daughter."

HUNTER

"We need to get back to the house, *now*," I say in a firm tone, and Blossom looks at me like a deer in the headlights for a moment. I'm already so focused on getting her and Flora to safety that I've forgotten that this is still a place of business, and of course, Blossom still has a job here. Her name tag with a hand-drawn blooming flower next to her name says as much.

"Excuse me, sir?" says a middle-aged woman who looks like a manager, making her way over to me with a wary look on her face. On her name tag it says *HELEN*. "Is there a problem I can help you with?"

"There's been an emergency," Blossom says quickly, coming to her senses and snapping into action. "I'm so sorry, but I have to go."

"What?!" the manager blurts, and I decide it's time for me to intervene.

"This is a *family* emergency," I say firmly, hugging Flora a little closer to me. "Someone very close to her has been in an accident, I need to get her to the hospital as soon as possible. You look like you have a full staff today. You can survive one morning without her, I hope."

"I…" the manager tries to protest, but the look I give her silences her. I look to Blossom, nod, and she hurries around the counter to follow us out.

Less than a minute later, we're in the car and driving.

"That was incredible," Blossom says as we pull off. "Have you always been that good at lying?"

"Must be a talent I learned I had when I started doing my work," I say casually. "Be ready for that in a year or so with her, by the way," I add, nodding back to Flora in the backseat. "She'll have gotten that from me. Sorry."

Blossom rolls her eyes, and I pull off onto the highway. I keep an eye on traffic, watching out for signs of our pursuer. I think I lost him on the way to the coffee shop, but I want to make sure before I lead us back to the house.

But I can't linger in traffic too long, either, because if the kidnapper thinks the house is unguarded, he might head there and run into Sage. I sincerely believe Sage is fully capable of killing a man, but she's still inexperienced enough that she might get hurt while doing so.

The drive home is tense. We don't want to discuss plans in front of Flora too much, but ignoring the elephant in the room is killing us. Instead, Blossom makes small talk with Flora about things that happened in her day before now. Flora humors her, but we can both tell that the kid is smart enough to know something isn't right, especially after what happened yesterday. Children are often smarter than we give them credit for.

Still, rather than going into the details of why we're taking her out of school for the day in order to avoid letting her get captured by a dangerous kidnapper, Blossom keeps the conversation light and friendly, asking her a few questions about what kinds of things Flora has been working on in school.

Finally, we get back to the house and hurry upstairs. When we unlock the door and barge in, I look across the living room and see Sage halfway to the door with a knife in her hand, which she quickly hides behind her back with wide eyes.

"Holy shit," she says, "you've got to warn me before you all come home like that!"

"Sorry, sorry," Blossom says, scooping Flora up in her arms and carrying her inside. "This was...kind of a rush."

"What's going on?" she asks, furrowing her brow.

"I got tailed on my way to Flora's school," I say

through a frown as I lock the door behind me, bolting every lock on the door. "So, work and school are cancelled today."

Sage's face goes pale, and she opens her mouth to speak, but she remembers Flora and just nods.

"Hey Flora, hun, you wanna go read some books in your room with me? We never finished the one about the boy in the boat."

"That one is so good!" Flora gushes immediately, and Blossom lets her down so she can run over to her sister, who takes the kid by the hand and gives us an understanding nod. She knows we need some time with Flora out of the room to figure things out.

"By the way," Sage adds before disappearing down the hall. "I think I can miss my shifts this week, if you need someone to guard the fort," she says with a nod to Flora.

"Thanks, Sage, that would be good," I say, and she disappears down the hall. I hear the door close a moment later, and Blossom and I both let out deep sighs.

"We need a plan," I say.

"We need literally *anything* more than what we've got right now," Blossom says, shaking her head and running her hands over her face as she makes her way into the kitchen. I'm just a few steps behind her. "Even if I were to go to the police right now, I couldn't give them anything solid. What could I say? 'Excuse me officer, I think someone's trying to steal my child. I have no idea what he looks like except that he's big and ugly and has a bird tattoo.'"

"You're right, that wouldn't be a good idea," I say, pacing. "Even if we had evidence, it would be too slow. We're dealing with someone who's trying to strike fast and get away faster. If he's not successful soon, chances are that he'll run off, but he'll be back. Someone who's already struck this much is persistent. You're positive there's nobody in your life who might come after you and her like this?"

"Nobody," she says, shaking her head. "Okay, here's an idea. Let's lay out all the information we know about him so far. Start chronologically, from the first thing that happened at the cabin."

"He broke in wearing all black, knowing people were inside, and he came armed," I say. "He's big and strong, and he's not bad at fighting. I would be willing to bet it's someone with military training, or some kind of armed forces like that. It sure as hell wasn't judo."

"Not doing a great job of making him seem like someone we can deal with," Blossom says. I chuckle.

"I said he was good at fighting, not that he was better than me. I mean it when I say I'll tear the bastard's head off, that's not an 'if' statement. Just got to catch the guy first."

"So, are we also sure he tracked us to the cabin?" she asks, sitting on the counter.

"Yes," I say. "When he first showed up, I was

willing to think he might just be some random burglar who came prepared and more desperate than most, but this has got to be the same guy each time. The chances of it being a coincidence are too slim."

"Agreed," she says, wringing her hands. "So, he was following us around Ithaca, and that's how he found us at the store."

I've already gotten a piece of paper and a pen out of a drawer and started writing up a map of all this information, nodding as she speaks.

"And he isn't just following us," she says, shuddering. "He was in Flora's room, so he *has* been in here. God, even this place isn't safe."

"It will be safe when I change the locks," I say as I write, not looking up, "but it'll be even safer when he's dead."

"He knows our schedule, knows how to get into our place, and knows my car," she says. "I...really don't want to get ahead of myself, because I know this whole 'true crime podcast' thing makes it *really* easy for me to sound crazy, but..."

"But this sounds like a professional," I finish for her, nodding in agreement.

"Okay, so I'm not crazy?"

"No," I say, frowning at the list I've written up. "It makes sense. And I know that's not comforting, but it tells us a little more about what we need to prepare for." I look up at her, watching her chew on her lip anxiously. "Hey, still with me?"

She gives her head a little shake, tucks a lock of hair behind her ear, and nods. "Sorry, it's just, I'm realizing I really, really don't like this kind of subject I've spent so much time on suddenly being so close to home."

"I'm sorry for that," I say, frowning. "But by the looks of things, it would have gotten this way even if I hadn't crossed paths with you by now."

"Oh no, I didn't mean it like-" she scrambles to backpedal, but I smile and hold up a hand.

"I hear you. But never mind all that, I think your skill set might be the useful one here."

"Seriously?" she asks, genuinely surprised.

"Crime podcaster. You've got an ear out to things like this all over the country, so let's think back. Kidnapper who cases his targets' houses before striking. He talks to acquaintances like that girl outside, finds out schedules, travel plans, habits, you name it. He's methodical. Probably spends time watching people and their homes before even thinking about making a move. Targets little girls. Based on what I've seen so far, this is definitely not his first time striking. He has experience. If I were a betting man, I'd say he has more than one victim in his past."

Blossom grimaces, but then she furrows her

brow. Hopping down, she hurries over to her laptop and starts pulling up a website I don't recognize.

"That fits a few profiles," she says, "but there was one that sounds not too far off from that I actually did a piece on recently. Guy fitting that description operating in rural Maine, believe it or not. The story came to the surface because one of his victims escaped."

"Escaped?" I say, stroking my beard as I look over her shoulder.

"Yeah, the guy has a bunker under his house. One of those safehouses in case nuclear war happens. They're all over the country. Apparently this girl of about Flora's age was taken and stashed there by a guy fitting that description. She only made it out because he didn't close it properly one day after a little too much drinking. The girl was smart enough to wait until he was long gone, and then she was brave enough to make a break for it. Police found her wandering down the interstate. It's a miracle she survived at all, a little girl that age. I mean, can you imagine? A child like Flora in that kind of situation. But they never found the house, so they had to dismiss the kid's testimony."

I hear every word she speaks, but I'm frozen, because it all clicked into place at the mention of a bunker in Maine.

"I know who he is," I growl, and Blossom pauses, then slowly looks up at me.

"You...what?"

I look down at her with fire in my eyes.

"I said I know who he is." I pace the room, running my hand over my face. How could I have been so stupid? How could I have repressed those memories so fiercely, even though it put the life of my own child in danger? Finally, I turn and face Blossom, who's looking at me with wide eyes.

"Back in Ithaca, I told Sage that I stayed with a real mean son of a bitch named Ronald. You were there to hear that, right?"

Her jaw drops, and I go on.

"I said I repressed parts of my memory, but now I know where I saw that fucking bird tattoo. It was on his arm. I found the bunker. He kept it out in a shed in the back where I wasn't allowed to go. He thought he did a slick job of keeping it secret from me, but I saw. I don't think he had anyone there while I lived with him. Too risky. When he wasn't beating my ass, he was drinking. I avoided him like the plague, but every now and then I caught a glimpse of that fucking tattoo. Did everything I could to forget that place. Called child services on him when he was passed out drunk one night, and that was that." I shake my head, pacing around more, feeling like my skin is crawling. "Can't believe that phone call literally saved my life. I was just happy enough he got blacklisted by foster services."

"Do you remember where that place is?" she asks

hurriedly, standing up and looking at me urgently. I turn to her and nod with a stony face.

"Oh, I remember. Memorized the address so I could tell the social workers." I take a few steps toward Blossom, looking at her intently and putting a hand on her shoulder. "Blossom, I know this isn't a new world for you, so what I'm about to ask you shouldn't come as a surprise. But we both know what needs to happen. I need to know if you're on board with that."

She locks eyes with me a long time before speaking again.

"Say it."

"Do I have your permission for one final kill? For Flora?"

She glares at me with more intensity than I've ever seen in those blue eyes of hers.

"For Flora? For our little girl? Hell. Fucking. Yes."

Hunter is behind the wheel of the car, his dark eyes set hard on the winding, twisting road in front of us. His hand reaches across the center console to gently pat my thigh in an attempt to reassure me. His palm is warm and dry on my leg, which I can't stop nervously jiggling. I don't normally think of myself as an especially jumpy, twitchy person, but this entire melodrama regarding Flora and the mysterious asshole who's stalking my family has me on edge. I can't stop fidgeting and biting my lip as I stare out the window. My own hands are icy cold and shaking. I slide one of them underneath Hunter's hand and he gives it a gentle squeeze, reminding me without a single word that no matter how terrifying this all seems, we're in it together. If there's one thing I can rely on Hunter to do, it's to protect me. To protect our family.

Because that's what it is, really: *our* family. Flora is our daughter, and both of us will spare any expense or effort to keep her safe from harm.

She's one of the truly good and innocent little souls in this dark world, and even if she weren't my baby, that kind of goodness is always worth protecting. That is one thing I have definitely picked up from Hunter and his perspective on the universe: that evil must be stamped out in order to establish a safer world for the good ones. If that means Hunter and I will have to sidestep into the shadows and occupy that uncomfortable, controversial gray space in between, then so be it. There was a time when I thought there was only black and white, good and bad-- that everyone and every act could be neatly categorized into those narrow, all-encompassing labels. But I know that's naive of me to assume. I get it now.

I was childish to ever think it was so easy to draw those lines in the sand. I once thought I would spend my entire life firmly in the light. I'd just keep my head up and do what I was taught is right, even when it's hard, even when it hurts. But sometimes it hurts too much. The thought of letting a beast like Ronald survive, free to stalk through the darkness on his bloodthirsty hunt for innocent lives to take and twist in his filthy hands is a thought I cannot abide. It cuts too deeply. I won't allow it. And neither will Hunter, especially now that we have started piecing together the full, hideous truth. This rabid animal of a man will never stop until he completes his evil mission. He will never stop looking for Flora. Ronald doesn't know how to cut his losses and move on. He will always come after her. And unless we want to spend the rest of our lives nervously looking over our shoulders, keeping Flora so sheltered and cooped up that she doesn't get to live the full, sunshiney life she deserves, we will have to put an end to him. To the evil he represents.

Hunter and I have never felt so close as we do right now. It's strange that when I first discovered his true identity, his reputation as the White Lilac killer, I lamented that it would be the wedge to drive us apart. I see now that, ironically enough, it will be the glue that keeps our family together. I abhor violence. I detest the idea of inflicting harm or pain on another living creature. But Hunter has taught me that sometimes, that's what has to happen. To maintain balance. To keep the world ever turning on its axis, to keep the good alive and well to see another day. Because what of life is worth it if all the goodness is perverted and broken and destroyed?

I understand him better than ever, and even though there has been a monumental shift between us, it's almost like we've gone back to who we used to be in some ways. Hunter and I used to lie under the lilacs and daydream about escaping our podunk town, about exacting revenge on those who had harmed us. The five years that lapsed between then and now hardly matter. It is just one long path leading us back home-- to each other.

And right now, it's also leading us to a more physical, literal home.

Early this morning, I rose out of bed to find Hunter already in the shower. Without a word, we cleaned up, got dressed, ate a simple, quick breakfast, and assured Sage we would be okay. We left her with Flora, which is one of the hardest things I've ever had to do. Flora was so sleepy, but she knew something was up. She's always been way more perceptive than anyone gives her credit for. She cried, begging for me to stay and play with her while Sage looked on helplessly. I promised her I would be back as soon as possible to play with her, and that promise is what's hanging on my mind. I know we are about to drive straight back into the gaping jaws of the beast we left behind years ago. I know it will be dangerous. I know there is a great chance that something will go wrong.

But I have to survive this. For Flora's sake.

So we headed out, getting on the road as early as we could manage. The first few hours were tense, but we still spoke occasionally, our tones hushed but full of love and promise. There's a heavy sense of camaraderie between us. We're partners in crime. Bonnie and Clyde, but with a much more positive mission. We're going to rid the world of one seriously fucked-up evildoer. And with every passing hour we inch closer and closer to the place where it all began. Every mile of Highway One fills me with dread.

"I haven't been back in five years," I murmur suddenly. "Not since my parents moved us to New York."

"I haven't been back either," Hunter replies. "Too many dark memories. You were the one bright spot in my time back in Weston. Once you were gone, well, there was nothing to tether me to the place."

The surroundings are beginning to look familiar now. The wide expanse of fields and trees, the rivers and lakes alongside the highway. The occasional cottage or rundown house set far back from the road on hills, as though they're glaring down at the highway with disgust. We pass by the sign for Weston, which still lists the population as just over two hundred. We see a sign for an old summer camp, probably long defunct by now. I feel sick to my stomach when the car whizzes past the entrance to the street where my childhood home probably still stands. I don't want to see it, I realize. I've left those memories far behind me, and that is exactly where they belong. I don't want my past to poison my future anymore.

"Do you know the way?" I ask quietly.

Hunter nods. "Yes. I could never forget--believe me, I have tried."

"So, let's go over what we know about our...our target," I suggest. "You start."

"Well," Hunter sighs, "I've kept loose files on my past foster parents and abusers over the years, just to keep tabs on them. A few years back, when I finally got enough information and courage together, I called social services and presented a case to have each and every one of my failed guardians removed from the foster service. I was successful, to my surprise. They all had their foster licenses revoked. Including Ronald."

"That's incredible, Hunter," I tell him honestly. "You didn't have to do any of that, because of your hard work, now other children won't be harmed by those assholes."

"Yeah. I only wish I could've nailed them sooner. Too many broken children passed through those homes. Far too many," he laments, shaking his head. "Anyway, I tried to keep an eye on the worst of them, just to make sure they didn't try anything else too horrific. But I guess I wasn't watching closely enough. Ronald slipped through the cracks. Probably because I'd done such a good job of repressing most of my memories regarding him. I wanted to just shove them so far down that they could never creep back up and hurt me again. But if there is one thing I've learned over the years, it's that no matter how deeply you bury a bad seed, it will eventually sprout up again."

"And when that happens, what do we do?" I ask him as the car turns down Dark Cove Road. We ride along in quiet for a moment as Hunter tries to regain his composure. I know he's rattled by how close we are to our destination.

Finally, he answers in a grim tone, "You have to reach down deep and rip it all out. Down to the very roots. You can't leave a single leaf or bud behind. Evil is like a weed. It grows fast and wild wherever you leave it, and it'll choke out all the good around it until you do the job right. That's what we're here to do tonight, Blossom. We're going to do the job right."

We have been driving all day, and dark is settling in around us as the car slowly, cautiously approaches the cabin Ronald treats as his headquarters. Clearly he doesn't spend all his time here, since he's been in Albany stalking Flora and me lately. But it's still his home. And Hunter is certain he'll be here. Like a beast retreating back to its lair.

"We're here," Hunter says softly. "The last foster home I ever lived in."

"Are you okay?" I ask, truly concerned. He shakes his head, still staring straight in front of us at the darkened property.

"No. I'm not," he admits. "But I will be. The second I know that evil son of a bitch is dead, I will be."

HUNTER

I never thought I would be coming back to this place.

Blossom and I crouch on a wooded hillside on the outskirts of the ragged house, staring at it from afar. One of the lights is on upstairs, and all the ones on the ground floor are out. It's late, so my guess is that he's upstairs either getting ready for bed or doing some other unsavory part of his evening ritual. I was never allowed upstairs. It was forbidden. When Ronald had me in his clutches, I was just starting to enter my teenage rebellion stage, one I've never really grown out of. But the one time I dared venture upstairs anyway, he caught me halfway up and gave me such a beating that I never thought about it again.

I look over to Blossom. Her face is shrouded in

darkness of the moonless night, but I can tell she's staring out at the house with a still, uneasy face. I reach over and squeeze her hand, and she looks to me.

"You okay?" I whisper.

"Yeah," she says softly. "It's just...Flora almost ended up in this place. I don't know if I believe in ghosts, but I get a really bad feeling around here."

"Like the air is angry," I say, nodding. "I felt it too. It kept me awake at night for weeks. The nightmares didn't leave me for a while, even after I left."

"What about you?" she whispers. "Are you okay?"

I'm silent for a few moments.

"This is my last kill," I say. "I can feel it. Even if you hadn't asked for it, there's a kind of finality to it. I feel like I'm tying up the last loose end. This...it's my past. They're the demons that haunted me when I was small. I'm ready to put them away for good."

"Hell yeah," she says, squeezing my hand.

"Hell yeah," I say back, squeezing hers. I nod toward the house, and we start moving forward.

I have my knife out. I never saw a gun in Ronald's house while I lived there, and he always struck me as the kind of guy who doesn't change his habits, but I can't be too careful. I almost tried to shake off Blossom, thinking it's too dangerous to have her here, but then I remember that this is closure for her, too. I wouldn't let some other asshole go and take care of this for me, so I can't expect Blossom to do so, either.

Besides, I know how to take care of my girl.

I stalk forward across the dark excuse for a yard in complete silence. Blossom is right at my side, just as skillful at moving quietly across the damp ground. I have to say, I'm impressed. She's a natural at this kind of thing.

But I stick out an arm to stop her as we get closer, and I look down under the faint light from the window up above to see the shining metal wire stretched out before us. It's a tripwire alarm. After pointing it out to Blossom, I carefully step over it and help her do the same. After that, I keep my eyes glued to the ground, scanning for any other traps he has in mind.

Once we get to the wall, I lead Blossom to one of the windows and peer inside. I see only darkness. The door to the upstairs room must be closed and locked. No light makes it down to the ground floor. If he's upstairs, that must mean he's busy. Any time he went up there, I couldn't hear a thing he was doing. That works to our advantage.

He never had alarms put in, thanks to his paranoia about anyone coming over to the house, so I feel confident as I carefully move the window back and forth until I get the latch open, and I slide it up as slowly as I can. It takes me almost a full two minutes to get it up quietly enough. After that, I use my knife to just as slowly and quietly cut open the screen.

I have a small flashlight in my pocket, and I decide to take a risk.

Clicking it on, I shine it into the house, just to be sure he isn't waiting for us in the darkness with a shotgun. Not being ready for surprises is how people get killed or caught. Watching the light illuminate the living room is indeed like a shot to the chest, but a very different kind.

I pan over the musty old couch I see myself curled up on, the doorway to the front I always dreaded him coming through, the little crawlspace under the stairs I tried to hide under so many times...

I click the light off and put it away. That's more than enough for now.

Carefully, I haul myself up and into the building as silent as a cat. Blossom comes next, and she's much easier for me to help get inside. Once in, I make sure my knife is at the ready as we move through the ground floor. I have a pretty good mental map of the place from my youth. Everything looks so eerily like I remember. It's like the place hasn't aged a day.

Fear sneaks up on you, trips you when you least expect it. It's devious, and it can turn the strongest of men into children again in the blink of an eye. I feel those daggers digging into the back of my spine as I make my way through the house with Blossom, entering the kitchen where so many yelling matches took place.

But I've had a lifetime of fear to train myself again. That's how I survived. I made fear my weapon, knowing that one day, I might just be able to turn it against my abusers. Iron sharpens iron, and I've made myself into something sharper and deadlier than anything I've ever run into.

The kitchen is also empty. Every time we reach a corner, I press myself against it and shine my light ahead of me to make sure we aren't about to run into a trap, and each time, it's just empty. One the ground floor is secure, I know it's time to head upstairs.

Leading Blossom over to the stairway, I steel my nerves. I stick to the side of the wall as I move up, remembering where each and every one of the creaky floorboards is. I reach the door take a deep, silent breath. Knife in one hand, I put my other on the doorknob, bracing myself. He lives alone now, so chances are that it's unlocked. I'm going to have to bank on that, because trying to pick the lock will alert him anyway. I can be quiet, but not that quiet-- especially when the whole house is so silent.

In a voice that's just barely above the faintest whisper, I count down so that Blossom is ready.

"Three...two...one."

I turn the knob and throw the door open, storming inside with my knife at the ready.

I'm greeted by silence.

But the scene within makes my mouth fall open, and as Blossom follows me in, her reaction is the same. Ronald isn't here. But everything else is.

This is his shrine.

The room is one big open square with no furniture but a single desk with a laptop on it. The walls themselves are far from empty, though. To the left and right, there are hundreds of pictures. All of them are of children, some clearly taken from social media, some taken in public. Each one of them is clustered together by person, each child with a dozen or so pictures. More disturbing still is just how many of them have large red Xs painted over each cluster.

Past victims.

"Oh my god," Blossom whispers. Her eyes are fixed on the pictures front and center of the room, just above the desk, surrounded by still-burning candles.

It's Flora.

There are more pictures of her up there than I can keep track of, some of them so recent that I recognize where they were taken. There are even pictures of the cabin where we stayed. I feel my hands shaking with anger as I step forward and look at her smiling face on so, so many of this maniac's pictures. I don't even want to touch the laptop. I want to drive a knife into it, but I know that it will be valuable evidence to use against him.

"I think I'm going to be sick," Blossom says, and I put a hand on her shoulder, checking behind us to make sure Ronald wasn't just waiting for a dramatic entrance.

"Me too," I growl. "And that's not all."

I point to the cluster of pictures of Flora, not far from it, I find the one cluster that doesn't match the pattern of all the rest.

It's me.

There are pictures of me from when I was a child, during the times I was living here under this monster's thumb. Some are from the early days, before I knew just how terrible he was, but some were from later. I feel a chill run down my spine as I realize some of them are pictures of me after I was taken from him.

All of them have my eyes cut out. There are incomprehensible scribbles on some of the photos, and I can take a few guesses at the gist of them.

I hug a shivering Blossom to me as we look at the ensemble with still faces. How can anything in life prepare you for something like this? To see not just your own child, but you yourself up on some psychopath's shrine?

"Obsessed is an understatement," I say, stepping forward and examining some of the photos. "No wonder he's been so relentless. Flora is the first time he's had this much real resistance. Realizing the coincidence that *I'm* involved too must have sent him over the deep end."

"He was already over the deep end," Blossom says, her voice quivering with anger and rage just barely contained. "This just brought out what was inside of him." Her eyes go wide, and she looks at me in a sudden panic. "We shouldn't have left Sage alone!"

I put a hand on her shoulder, shaking my head.

"Don't worry about that," I say. "The door was unlocked and the candles are still burning. This was a setup. I should have known he wouldn't be here. He just wanted us to see this. Wanted *someone* to see this. Hell, if he's this unstable, he probably wants to get caught. That would explain why he got so sloppy. And we can use that to our advantage. We can end this."

"But if he's not here, where is he?"

I turn and look out the window, where I see the light cast on the only other place on the property: the shed, where the bunker entrance is. Blossom follows my gaze, and her face goes pale. She puts a hand over mine on her shoulder, looks at me resolutely, and she nods.

Five minutes later, I'm kicking the door of the shed open. I'm done sneaking around. I've seen our daughter on the wall of a serial killer's lair, and I'm out for blood.

The shed is small, and there's only one remarkable feature in the middle of the room: a hatch leading down to the bunker. And the hatch is open. Of course it is.

"He's waiting for us," I say, narrowing my eyes. I don't bother to lower my voice anymore. Knife ready, I take Blossom's hand and make my way down into what feels like the descent to the underworld.

The steps don't creak. They're made of solid concrete. There's a light down below, and as I walk toward it, I get more confident that I know what I'm walking into.

"You already know it's over," I call down below. "Why even bother with all this?"

That familiar voice answers me as we see him, and it sends a chill up my spine.

"It feels right, somehow."

The bunker is hauntingly simple. If I didn't know better, I'd think I was just walking into someone's legitimate hideout, somewhere a paranoid person might keep a little shelter tidy and prepared just on the off-chance of a nuclear apocalypse. There's a bed, a lot of cabinet space for canned goods, and a little counter space with a can opener to make it come together. There's also a table with a single chair at it, and sitting at that chair is a man I wish I'd never see again in my life.

Ronald is sitting there, wearing a big coat, sweatpants, and sneakers, looking smug and drunk. There's a machete on the table, and his hand is on it, gently stroking the sharp edge before coming to a rest at the handle.

"Hunter," he says, staring at me. His face is emotionless. No remorse, no fear, nothing. Blossom holds her ground beside me, glaring at him, and I can almost feel her blood boiling. Ronald's eyes flick between us, and he cracks a smile.

"I really can't tell you how glad I am you two happened to be together," he says. "Pure serendipity. It made playing with you all the more entertaining."

"How long have you kept this up?" Blossom hisses.

"Long enough," he replies quickly. His eyes linger on Blossom, and I feel furious that he dares to even look at her. "How's Flora?"

"Shut the fuck up," I growl, stepping forward. He doesn't budge. "One more word about her out of your mouth, and I'll cut your tongue out."

But his eyes are locked onto Blossom. "I like to think he gets that anger from me, you know," he says. "It pleases me to know you got to see what he's really like. Father of your child. Yes, I did the math. You two have quite a history together. I never had a child of my own, but now, I feel like something of a parent to Hunter here. It certainly wasn't a happy upbringing that made him so good at avoiding my sights all these years. The one who got away," he adds, smiling at me. "When he kills me, what difference do you think there is between the two of us, hm?"

"Save that crap," Blossom says, stepping forward with clenched fists. "Hunter is nothing like you. I knew it before we got torn apart, and I know it now, even after everything I know about him. You think I don't pay attention to the way monsters like you think? You're narcissists who can't get enough of playing with human life. I think you're even jealous of the children you kill."

That seems to hit a little too close to home, and I see Ronald's mouth twitch. His eyes roll over to me.

"You've got a feisty one on your hands," he says. "She probably rehearsed that, in case she ever met one of the killers like us she likes to prattle about. Shame you didn't stay with me. I could have taught you a lot, if you'd shown potential."

"Don't worry, I learned plenty from you," I say. "I learned what to look for in my prey."

"You two have such fun little comebacks," he says, his mouth splitting into a hideously mild laugh. He pauses, then looks thoughtful. "I wonder if Flora will be as lively?"

His hand wraps around his machete, and he lurches up far more quickly than either of us thought him capable of. His face looks more like a demon's than a man's. He lunges for me, arm raised as he crosses the small room.

And at the same time, I flip the knife upside-down, bring it back, and let it fly from my hand, right toward him.

He hasn't even hit the ground before I've taken out the last lilac I'll ever place.

It has been one hell of an eight months.

I lean back in my chair, groaning in relief as I shut the laptop in front of me. I feel satisfied. I've just finished two more chapters in the saga of the White Lilac Killer, the book that I've finally gotten around to writing. Just a few more, and I'll have a workable draft to send off to editing.

I hear footsteps behind me, and I let my head fall back enough to look behind me upside-down, where I see Hunter walking toward me, still in uniform after getting home from work just ten minutes ago.

"Hey there, bestseller," he says in a husky voice as he slides his hands over my shoulders and starts to rub them. "How'd it go?"

"Just finished for the day, I think," I say with a relieved sigh. "I'm dreading having to work on the ending, honestly."

"Is the publisher still giving you trouble about changing the ending?" he asks.

"Yeah, and I'm not sure what to tell him," I say. "You and I both know the White Lilac Killer died back in Maine. I didn't think I'd have to play fiction writer for real, but I think we can come up with something good."

"I agree," he says, leaning down and kissing me on the head before sliding his arms further down…

…and over my swollen, pregnant belly.

We framed Ronald back in Maine, arranging the scene so that it looked like he'd killed himself and been the White Lilac Killer all along. I still don't know entirely how Hunter pulled that off, but it fooled police reports. He evaded public attention, leaving Flora and I to be the ones who survived him.

As soon as that blew over, we packed up and moved out here to Lancaster, New Hampshire, and Hunter's new job set us up in this house that I don't have a single complaint about. It's a quaint little Victorian style house in a soft baby blue color with white trim that looks like a dollhouse come to life.

The perfect place to wait for our second child to come.

And it wasn't long after finding out that our son was on the way that Hunter put a ring on my finger. He said he'd been planning it since we escaped the hell-house in Maine, and finding out about the pregnancy just felt like it was the right time.

Besides, his new job as superintendent at White Mountain National Forest means we're going to be stable and steadier than ever...and I've finally had time to get my true crime podcast off the ground.

He kisses me on the cheek, and that kiss turns into several more all up and down the side of my neck, and by the time he has me blushing and laughing, he takes my hands and stands me up. I look up at him, unable to stop smiling, and I know the look on his face. He runs his hands over my swollen belly, then moves them around to my ass and gives it a squeeze as he pulls me closer to him. He kisses me on the lips this time, so deeply that I sigh into him, feeling warmth spread all over my body.

He brings my hand up to his mouth, and he kisses the massive engagement ring on my finger, smiling at me.

"What do you say, bride-to-be?" he asks. "I think you've earned some relaxation."

Less than a minute later, I'm giggling like a teenager again as I roll back onto the bed, and he slides my comfy pants off my legs. I crawl backward as he exposes my legs and my pussy, a hungry look in his eyes as he pulls the flowing maternity shirt off me, tossing it aside and leaving me naked before him. Something about being so exposed while he's in uniform thrills me, and he seems to like it too.

He runs his hands over my body, and I shiver, feeling him savoring every inch of me. I squirm on the bedsheets, reveling in how soft and comfortable everything feels. Clean sheets, a fresh room, and a rugged man who smells like rich earth and pine-- I don't know what I did to deserve a guy like Hunter, but whatever it was, I want to keep doing it.

We have to be more gentle now that I'm so swollen I feel like I'm going to pop at any second, but that hasn't made the bedroom any less exciting. His hands grope my hips, then slide up and down my thighs as he kisses me all over. Anywhere there's exposed skin, I feel his lips and the ruggedness of his beard brushing over me, making me tingle and feel so, so warm in the way only he can do.

I let my head fall back, running my hands through my hair as I stretch out, and a moment later, I feel his tongue on my pussy. I let out a gasp as he starts licking me, hands clutching my hips and scooting me back into a more comfortable position as he crawls onto the bed. I feel like I'm a reward being devoured after a hard day's work, both for him and for me. His tongue massages my pussy in long, strong strokes that end in some much-needed attention to my clit.

Writing this book has been a passionate experience, both because I just like writing about the man I know to be my lover, and because I didn't omit the parts of it that got a little less than family-friendly. Fortunately, Hunter is always here to scratch that itch.

His tongue works my pussy relentlessly. Each time the tip of his tongue kisses my clit, I feel my heart pound faster, every nerve in my body enjoying the warm waves of bliss pulsing through me. I was already wet when he carried me to the bedroom, and now, I'm all the more excited. Being so uninhibited is beyond freeing.

It's perfect.

Over and over again, his tongue makes me squirm, but his hands are so strong and firm that I can't escape him. I'm a prisoner to his attention, and I feel myself getting tighter the more he works me. I reach forward and run my hands through his short hair, feeling his head as he devours me. I'm so wet that I can hear him down there, and it's both embarrassing and wonderfully exciting all at once. I feel like I'm indulging myself more than I deserve, no matter how much Hunter tells me I deserve it.

It doesn't take long for me to give that telltale gasp. Ever since Hunter pointed out that he can tell when I'm about to come, I've gotten more embarrassed every time I start to. He thinks it's cute, though, and I can't get enough of the way he looks at me when he knows I'm squirming in his hands.

I bring my hands down to the sheets and clutch them as I feel my whole body getting ready to release. The next moment, I let out a long, desperate sigh, arching my back as the fire in my pussy spreads out to the rest of my body. It's utter bliss, and I let myself smile with my eyes closed while Hunter gives me one last, long lick up my pussy before standing up on his knees.

He unzips his pants and moves forward, releasing that massive cock of his and stroking it while I crack my eyes open to look up at him and the pillar he holds over me.

"I love you," his thick voice growls as he perches his cock on my lower lips.

"I love you so fucking much," I breathe desperately, just a second before he penetrates me.

His cock goes in deep, and since my orgasm hasn't even finished yet, I whimper and shudder wonderfully as I feel his bulging, eager cock burying itself into me. I feel his rough clothes against my thighs as he picks my legs up and starts rutting into me. He's gentle at first, rocking back and forth to ease me into the action.

It's almost funny, seeing such a huge, powerful, aggressive man being so careful around my pregnant stomach. But he loves every second of it. Even being gentle and showing restraint, it's just another way to show me that he loves me. And he doesn't just love me-- he loves the family that we've made together.

The ring on my finger is the only piece of 'clothing' I have on right now, and I never want to take it off unless I have to. Something about that visual symbol of our togetherness fills me with such a warm feeling that my heart does a somersault whenever I'm close to him.

That means that when he's inside me, it's pure, uninhibited bliss.

He gets faster as he finds a comfortable pace, sliding his cock in and out of me with hip and ab muscles that have only gotten stronger over time. He's always looking for ways to perfect himself for me-- those are his words, not mine.

He reaches further under my ass and hoists me up, angling me so he can get to an even better angle and start pounding into me the way he knows I love it. His cock is so long and thick that it fills every space inside of me better than I could have ever dreamed. It's easy to lose myself in the feeling, letting my arms fall back and just pushing up my hips as much as I can to help him along. He insists on it being that way. He doesn't want a pregnant woman having to go through too much trouble, even in bed, and I'm in no rush to argue.

Besides, once this last month is over, I'm going to make it well worth his while.

I feel him pulse inside me, and I know there's a bead of precum spilling into me, mixing with my honey and letting me know that he's soon going to be letting all that pent-up tension out on me soon. Every sensation in my body feels so much more intense when he's in me. He's a storm of passion every time he touches me, and it never seems to end.

The bulging tip of his cock is grinding against the innermost depths of my pussy. It feels different almost every day now, thanks to the growing baby inside me. It's a subtle difference, but it's there. In fact, I kind of like it, more than I expected to like it. Everything feels more tight, but thanks to how wet he gets me any time he starts touching me, it doesn't make it any harder. He feels bigger than ever, and he's already huge.

More importantly, he knows how to use it.

His thrusting gets faster, and I watch his whole body moving like one perfect machine to fuck deep into me, pistoning with such precision that I feel the warmth in my body starting to crest up again. It's like every part of me is being strung back, ready for release, and it's such a warm and overwhelming feeling that I can do absolutely nothing to stop it. He has me impaled on his cock, and every time the rim of the crown of his cock slides through my wet pussy, I want him to just keep going.

I lose track of time, gripping the sheets and clenching my eyes as the feelings get almost too strong to bear. But soon, I realize he's losing his focus and going wild. I feel more precum spurt out of him, and I know he's about to reach his peak.

I bite my lip, bracing myself as I feel tighter and tighter under my belly, and finally, I let out a long, sweet gasp as I feel warmth spread out through my whole body at the same time that he comes. His hot cock releases spurt after spurt of healthy, virile seed, the same seed that put our second child in me.

In that heightened state mid-orgasm, all I can think about is Hunter. The look on his face, the way he touches me, the feeling of his rippling muscles under my fingertips, it's all too much to resist. Finally, it comes to an end, and reality seeps back into the room while he's still lodged in me, panting and satisfied.

I open my eyes to look up at his loving face, and he leans down slowly, scooping my head into his hand and kissing me deeply. We lose ourselves for just another moment until he pulls out of me slowly and smiles.

"Let's get you cleaned up."

I step out of the shower just in time to hear the school bus outside.

We hurry to throw some clothes on, and Hunter leads the way, hurrying downstairs to open the front door. Flora comes racing inside just in time, right into Hunter's arms, and he picks her up and hugs her, laughing.

"Daddy!" she gushes as he swings her around, laughing.

"Hey now, what about me?" I tease, putting my hands on my hips as I approach the two.

"You gotta beat him to the door, Mommy!" she

says, laughing as he kisses her head and lets her back down. She's too big to be picked up very regularly, but that doesn't stop Hunter. I have a feeling he'll be doing that until she gets into her rebellious phase, and then he'll surprise her and start up again when she chills out in her twenties.

Oh god, nevermind, I don't want to think that far in the future yet!

"Come on," Hunter says, gesturing for Flora to follow him toward the back door. "I've got something to show you."

"What is it?" she asks as she trots after him, and I follow along, beaming at the two.

"You'll see!"

We step out onto the yard, where Flora wastes no time in running out at full tilt and going in circles while Hunter crosses the yard to the lilac tree in the middle of the back yard, and before he even points it out to Flora, I can see why he's excited.

"Here, look," he says as Flora runs up to him, and he scoops the girl up into his arms and holds her up to the foliage.

"Flowers!" she says excitedly as I come up beside them.

"Yep," he says, chuckling. "Blue lilacs. They're just starting to bud. They'll be blossoming in a few days, we should keep an eye on them."

Flora looks absolutely fascinated, and I can't help but smile at it before nudging Hunter.

"So," I say, "Mr. Symbolism, if you liked white lilacs for the innocence, what do blue lilacs mean?"

He laughs and looks at me lovingly, peering into my eyes for a long moment before answering.

"Tranquility," he says in a soft tone. "And happiness."

This is the happiest day of my life.

And let me tell you, with the way things have been going over the past year or so, that's a pretty big statement to make. Because my life is good. No, it's amazing. I'm currently standing at the altar in front of the most handsome, clever, brave, selfless man in the world. He's gazing down at me with something almost like tears sparkling in those gorgeous brown eyes, and I know I should be listening to what the priest is saying, but it's hard to focus on anything except for the love thumping like crazy in my heart. It's finally happening. We're getting married.

Behind me are my two bridesmaids, the most important women in my life. My sister Sage looks radiant with her hair elaborately twisted up into an elegant bun. For once, she's let a real makeup artist do her makeup, and she didn't even balk at the dress I picked out for her: a sapphire-blue, floor-length gown with intricate beading. Wearing the same dress but a long, flowy braid instead of a bun, is Samantha, standing next to her. As it turns out, Sam has been quite the busy little bee, finding a job, a place to rent, and getting her GED. Sage and Samantha have grown closer, since they still live in Albany. Last month, they got an apartment together and are helping each other get through classes. Sometimes it can be hard being away from them, since Hunter, the kids, and I all live in New Hampshire. But we Skype almost every day, and we visit as much as possible. It's truly a blessing to have them here for our special day.

On the other side of the altar, behind Hunter, are his groomsmen. Hunter has always led a solitary lifestyle, so it's new for him to finally have a real group of friends. He met these guys at his job working in the national park. Their names are Travis and Will, and they're exactly the kind of outdoorsy, rugged, lumberjack-esque types that make the girls swoon.

Well, not me, of course. Because they may be great, but I've landed the best man of all: the boy I have loved since I was eighteen years old, since the first time I caught him hopping our fence while I was picking berries. Since we first lay under the lilacs together, kissing and daydreaming about some distant, beautiful future. Well, that future is now.

We're here. We've made it!

Standing off to the side a little, holding Sage's hand, is Flora. I'm amazed at how she's been able to keep quiet and well-behaved throughout the marriage ceremony. But that was the bargain; I promised her she could be the flower girl if she promised to be good. It worked. She's been a perfect angel the whole time. Still, I'm kind of hoping the priest will hurry things along-- I'm eager to get past all the ceremonial stuff and just kiss my new husband already.

Especially because there's another little one struggling to keep quiet: our baby son, Forrest. Samantha, bless her, is holding him during the vows. She keeps having to rock him back and forth to keep him from getting cranky. Overall, he's an angel baby; he rarely cries for long, and he's got this thousand-watt smile that could melt even the coldest heart. I can't wait to spend my life with Hunter, raising our little family and watching our kids grow up close and happy. I'm even thinking about getting licensed to work in child care and development, with hopes of Hunter and I eventually getting our foster licenses. We want to provide the service he was so cruelly denied. We want to be good parents, to offer a warm and happy home to children who so desperately need one. It's a lot to take on, but with Hunter by my side, nothing is impossible.

Finally, the priest says, "You may kiss your bride."

My heart is pounding so hard it feels like it might burst as Hunter, the love of my life, the prince charming I've dreamed of for years, leans in to kiss me softly at first, then with a little more passion. I know it's probably not super appropriate for church, but what can I say? We can't help ourselves. He takes me by the hand and leads me down the aisle as our well-wishers stand up and applaud, tossing little white flowers over us as we pass. Once we all spill out onto the grassy lawn of the little white chapel with the red door, the festivities begin.

"You ready to mingle?" I ask my new husband with a giggle.

He rolls his eyes, a grin on his face. "If we must. But you know what I'm really looking forward to?"

"What?" I ask, already pretty sure I know the answer.

He leans in to whisper in my ear, "The honeymoon."

I giggle and nod. "Yep. Me, too. But first, we mingle."

"Yes, ma'am," Hunter replies. "Whatever you say, wifey."

I can't help but beam at the new nickname. It's hard to let go of him for even a moment, but we spend the rest of the lovely afternoon chatting with wedding guests. We play with Flora and Forrest. We talk with Sam and Sage. Hunter commiserates about work with his groomsmen, and then he shares a sweet, poignant moment with two guests we weren't sure would attend: two of the former foster siblings Hunter had growing up. During the ceremony, they stood in the back with tears in their eyes, happy to see that little Hunter has grown up to be such a fine, successful, happy man. And I know they must be overjoyed to know that the monster who made their childhoods a living hell, that bastard Ronald, is no more.

In fact, everyone's pretty damn relieved to have him out of the world. My book about the White Lilac killer has been a massive success, and because I pinned all of Hunter's work on him, he got to die in hated infamy. There are talks about my book possibly being turned into a movie at some point, but Hunter and I are still on the fence about that. For now we're just happy to leave the past in the past, especially since we have such a bright and shining future to look forward to now. Together. As it should be.

At the end of the evening, when the music is playing, Hunter and I dance slowly and closely on the green. We spin and hold each other, glowing with love and fulfilment. "This is everything I ever wanted," I whisper to him, holding back happy tears.

He kisses me softly on the cheek. "You are everything I've ever wanted. And I've known that since the first day we met, since the first time we held each other underneath a branch of these," Hunter says. He pulls a tiny sprig of white lilac from his coat pocket and gently tucks it into my hair. I'm so surprised and touched that I can't keep the happy tears from falling. Grinning up at him, I see my whole world. My whole heart.

"There was a time when I thought I was too far gone to find love," he admits. "I thought I was too broken. That I would have to be alone. That I would never be good enough for a woman like you. But Blossom, you have given me back my happiness. My innocence. Everything that was stolen from me, you've returned to me tenfold."

"And you have given me hope. You've shown me that I am strong, that I deserve the kind of love I thought only happened in dreams. You seemed too good to be true, but here we are now, and nothing has changed except the world around us. I love you, Hunter. I loved you then and I love you now more than ever," I murmur.

My husband looks into my eyes, softly and adoringly, and replies, "And I love you, my wife. Now and forever."

Killing For Her

Abducted

Stepbrothers:

Ruthless

Criminal

Standalones:

Betting on Love

Hunter's Baby

I Hired A Hitman

Vegas Boss

Rock Hard Bodyguard

Innocence For Sale: Jane

Redeeming Viktor

Romance:

Falling for her Boss (Novella)

Most Wanted: Lilly (Novella)

Bound as the World Burns (SFF)

Erotic Thriller:

The Dangerous Men Series:

The Narrow Path

Strayed from the Path

Path to Ruin

Alexis Abbott is a Wall Street Journal & USA Today bestselling author who writes about bad boys protecting their girls! Pick up her books today if you can't resist a bad boy who is a good man, and find yourself transported with super steamy sex, gritty suspense, and lots of romance.

She lives in beautiful St. John's, NL, Canada with her amazing husband.

facebook.com/abbottauthor

twitter.com/abbottauthor

instagram.com/alexisabbottauthor

bookbub.com/authors/alexis-abbott

pinterest.com/badboyromance

youtube.com/AlexisAbbott

ACKNOWLEDGMENTS

Thank you to my amazing Patrons. I'm constantly humbled and grateful for your support.

Ramona Cabrera
Melissa Hedrick
Virginia Swanson
Dawn Daughenbaugh
Don Doss
Stacie Currie

If you'd like to join them — and get my ebooks or paperbacks — you can find me here on Patreon.
https://www.patreon.com/alexisabbott